"I Want You, Charly,"

Burt groaned softly, openly admitting his need.

Against all common sense Charlene explored the smooth contours of his chest and then moved to caress his bare shoulders and the tense muscles in his back.

"Burt, *please*," she said in a voice that held as much longing as reluctance.

Then she realized that if she didn't stop things now, at once, it would be too late.

"No!" she burst out, twisting out of his arms.

"How foolish of me to be so presumptuous," he said with cutting irony. "Things really haven't changed, have they, Charly? You can't bring yourself to make love with an ordinary man, but you still have to make every man want you."

CAROLE HALSTON
is the wife of a sea captain, and she writes while her husband is out at sea. Her characters often share her own love of nature and enjoyment of active outdoor sports.

Dear Reader:

Silhouette has always tried to give you exactly what you want. When you asked for increased realism, deeper characterization and greater length, we brought you Silhouette Special Editions. When you asked for increased sensuality, we brought you Silhouette Desire. Now you ask for books with the length and depth of Special Editions, the sensuality of Desire, but with something else besides, something that no one else offers. Now we bring you SILHOUETTE INTIMATE MOMENTS, true romance novels, longer than the usual, with all the depth that length requires. More sensuous than the usual, with characters whose maturity matches that sensuality. Books with the ingredient no one else has tapped: excitement.

There is an electricity between two people in love that makes everything they do magic, larger than life—and this is what we bring you in SILHOUETTE INTIMATE MOMENTS. Look for them this May, wherever you buy books.

These books are for the woman who wants more than she has ever had before. These books are for you. As always, we look forward to your comments and suggestions. You can write to me at the address below:

Karen Solem
Editor-in-Chief
Silhouette Books
P.O. Box 769
New York, N.Y. 10019

CAROLE HALSTON
The Marriage Bonus

Silhouette Special Edition
Published by Silhouette Books New York

America's Publisher of Contemporary Romance

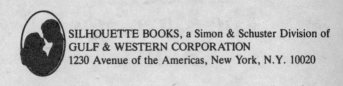
SILHOUETTE BOOKS, a Simon & Schuster Division of
GULF & WESTERN CORPORATION
1230 Avenue of the Americas, New York, N.Y. 10020

ISBN: 0-671-53586-2

First Silhouette Books printing April, 1983

10 9 8 7 6 5 4 3 2 1

Map by Ray Lundgren

America's Publisher of Contemporary Romance

Printed in the U.S.A.

Other Silhouette Books by Carole Halston

Stand-in Bride
Love Legacy
Keys to Daniel's House
Undercover Girl
Collision Course
Sunset in Paradise

Chapter One

The trip was an inspiration in so many ways. Charlene really did look forward to seeing Cappy again. It had been at least three years since she'd managed to get back to Louisiana for a visit, she realized with a grimace of dismay. Life could become so complicated; one could neglect important people. Goodness knows no one had been more important in her life than Cappy. She'd always called him that, like everybody else did, even though he was her grandfather.

Grandparents were usually depicted in advertising as being elderly, doddering people. Cappy had never fit that image to Charlene—always "Charly" to Cappy. She could see him clearly in her mind's eye as she headed south on Interstate 85 out of Atlanta. A short, squat man with a grizzled beard and piercing brown eyes narrowed into a permanent squint, he looked every inch the average person's concept of a sea captain. Actually, Cappy had never been a captain on ships, but rather on tugboats on the Mississippi River, and rarely outside the state of Louisiana. He was a born storyteller and had many colorful tales to entertain the listeners who invariably gathered around him, some of them having already heard the stories many times before.

Charlene's mouth curved into a reminiscent smile as she visualized Cappy sitting back in his chair on the fuel dock at the marina, methodically loading his pipe with tobacco, with a faraway look in his eyes. Someone, perhaps Charly herself, had just prompted him: "Hey, Cappy, tell them about the time . . ."

The man she could see so vividly was neither young nor old. He was ageless. He was simply Cappy, the warm, wonderful person who had welcomed her when she came to live with him for a year when she was twelve. That year had stretched into eight years after her parents were killed by a terrorist's bomb in the South American country where her father had taken a one-year assignment overseeing a drilling rig. She had lived with Cappy until she and Paul were married.

And though it was true she had been too caught up in her own life as the wife of an up-and-coming young corporate man to visit Cappy often during the last ten years, he had always been there in her thoughts. She might forget him for brief stretches of time, but he occupied a permanent, central importance in her life. Cappy was a constant, an anchor, that one person in the world everyone needs—the person who would love her and be concerned about her well-being no matter what she did. She could be a modern-day Benedict Arnold and betray her country, and though Cappy would sternly disapprove, he would still love her. She *knew* that without his ever having told her in so many words.

And now Cappy had had a stroke . . .

That news had struck her to the core more than Paul's shamefaced announcement two weeks ago that he was in love with another woman and would be moving out of the house to live with her. It was only as she heard the words that Charlene realized she had been expecting something of the kind. Her relationship with Paul had not been all that it should have been for the better part of a year, but she had been ignoring all the telltale signs: the frequent business trips out of town, the working late at the office, the telephone calls at the last minute explaining he had to take an important client out to dinner or out for cocktails. When he did arrive at home, he was too tired to be interested in sex.

Charlene had been through marriage breakups with so many of her friends through the last few years that her own had a weird familiarity. But there was nothing familiar about Cappy's being ill, and though he had been offhanded about the stroke when she talked to him on the telephone—insisting it was a "mild" stroke, just a warning according to the doctor—she had to see for herself that Cappy was all right.

Aside from her genuine concern for him, the

timing for the visit was perfect. Getting away from Atlanta now would give her a chance to gain some perspective on her life, on the breakup of her marriage. By the time she returned, the gossip would have settled down. By then there would probably be another victim to the vicissitudes of matrimony: another of her friends or acquaintances would have been deserted by a husband or left a husband herself for one reason or another. All of those reasons were familiar to Charlene by now. How many times had she heard someone joke or even said the glib words herself: "There must be a divorce bug going around! Sure hope *I* don't catch it!" It was sad that in modern society divorce was so common it was treated casually, like an attack of the flu.

Had she wanted to push herself, she could have made the drive from Atlanta to her destination in south Louisiana, just north of New Orleans, in one long haul, but instead she broke the trip up into two days, wanting to arrive in the early afternoon of the second day and not be totally exhausted. Cappy lived on the premises of the small marina he owned and operated a few miles upriver from the tiny hamlet of Madisonville, nestled on the western bank of the Tchefuncte River. Visitors to that section of south Louisiana were intrigued with tongue-twister names of Indian derivation like *Tchefuncte.*

Charlene took an exit off Interstate 10 at Slidell because she wanted to drive through Mandeville on Highway 190 and see her old stomping grounds. Because of the school districting, she had gone to

Mandeville schools rather than to the little Madison-ville school, even though the latter would have been closer in distance. She knew now that it had been just plain luck she had attended Mandeville High and associated with the kind of people who had been her closest friends there, the offspring of successful executives and professional people, not the children of locals who had lived in Louisiana for generations. Had Cappy's marina been located a few miles further downriver and on the Madisonville side of the river, her whole life might have been drastically different. Chances were good that she would have married one of the local boys instead of somebody like Paul, who was destined to go places and be successful.

Even with divorce facing her after ten years of marriage, she had no regrets for having chosen the life she'd enjoyed as his wife and still preferred to live. It was unappealing to think of living any other way, and she hadn't given up completely on salvaging her marriage yet, for in her opinion it was well worth salvaging.

To her consternation she found that great changes had taken place in the whole Mandeville area since her last visit. It was fast losing its quaint rural atmosphere. Shopping centers had sprung up almost everywhere she looked, and she almost got lost in the complicated maze of new highways and intersections. Evidently urban sprawl from New Orleans had spilled across the twenty-four miles of the Lake Pontchartrain Causeway to St. Tammany Parish.

An objective passenger in Charlene's car might

have found her indignation amusing under the circumstances. She had lived most of the last ten years in fast-growing boom cities like Atlanta and Houston, but she was appalled at the evidence of growth and change she saw everywhere around her, even on the stretch of two-lane highway between Mandeville and the turnoff to the marina, approximately two miles short of the drawbridge across the Tchefuncte River. *The whole damned area would soon be one gigantic subdivision!* she fretted in disgust and then consoled herself that at least the marina would be the same.

It never changed even though Cappy was always making little repairs, such as replacing pieces of tin that had blown off the roofs of the covered slips. The creosoted pilings stood a little askew as though they had been driven by a tipsy giant, and the planked docks were not even, presenting something of a hazard to the unsure foot, but the overall effect was rustic and charming to those who preferred "character" to the sterile regularity of concrete piers like those in city marinas.

Charlene's anticipation grew stronger as she turned right off the highway onto the shell-covered road that wound back to the marina. She heard the grumble of heavy machinery before she could see the source of the sound. Her sense of betrayal was overwhelming as she drove into the marina and saw the beehive of activity in progress. A huge monster of a machine was pulling up the old pilings and driving down new ones that were perfectly rounded instead of looking hand-hewn like the old ones. A crew of men were also tearing up the old piers and rebuilding them.

Braking, she sat behind the wheel of her smart little Audi sedan and stared, aghast. Her sense of horror couldn't have been greater if she had arrived at her home in Atlanta from a routine shopping trip and discovered the presence of grotesque aliens from another planet. This was awful! Cappy's marina was being *ruined!* The new pilings already driven into place all looked exactly alike and were placed at precise distances apart. The portions of rebuilt piers had a geometric regularity she found appalling. *Who was responsible for this?* she wondered.

Clutching the steering wheel with hands that actually trembled, Charlene slowly accelerated and drove through the marina toward the river, her mind a jumble of questions and protests. Had Cappy sold the marina without telling her? She couldn't imagine that he could afford the kind of renovation going on. It must be expensive to hire a work crew like that one, not to mention the cost of the huge pile driver and the bulldozers she saw in operation.

Why did this have to be happening now of all times? She was so looking forward to returning to the place she thought of as changeless. To discover that the marina was undergoing such drastic renovation was almost more than she could bear.

Realizing that she was overreacting, Charlene made an effort to compose herself as she parked her car in front of Cappy's house. Thank God that at least looked the same. It was still a weathered silvery gray, the cypress boards having never been painted or stained. Like the building adjoining it, which housed the office and store, the house was built on pilings and jutted out over the edge of the water. Charlene had always loved the sound of rain on the tin roof, especially at night when she was snuggled into bed.

Throat aching with unshed tears, Charlene got out of the car and mustered a smile. It wouldn't do for her to greet Cappy looking as though she had just attended a funeral.

"Anybody home?" she called loudly, slamming the door of her car harder than necessary.

Cappy appeared almost immediately in the open doorway of the store, a broad smile on his face.

"Charly!" he yelled, managing to make her old nickname the warmest possible welcome. In one hand he held the inevitable pipe and perched atop his head at a rakish angle was the Greek fisherman's cap, black and narrow-brimmed, that he always wore. It enhanced his appearance of the typical sea captain.

Charlene took several running steps and threw her arms around his neck in a quick, hard hug before standing back to look at him.

"Oh, Cappy! It's so good to see you!" she exclaimed huskily, managing to hold back the tears. If she started crying, she was afraid she would not be able to stop.

"Good to see you, girl," he said gruffly, bringing the pipe up and clamping it between his teeth. "Hope you came to stay awhile. Might as well get your things in while we're out here."

Charlene followed him around to the trunk of her car and unlocked it, needing every second she could get to bring her emotions under control. It had been bad enough arriving at the marina and seeing the changes taking place in it, but far more appalling was the sight of Cappy's face. Time had finally begun to take its toll on him, or else some protective lens had been stripped away from her eyes. *Cappy was getting old!* There were more lines now, but it was more than that. His flesh had begun to sag around the eyes and nose and mouth.

A cold numbness had begun to settle in Charlene's bones and joints. With considerable effort she managed to answer Cappy's routine questions about her trip from Atlanta, but underneath she was thinking, *Dear God, Cappy is getting old!* The realization brought her shockingly face to face with human mortality for the first time. She knew everybody had to die eventually, herself as well as Cappy, but knowing that intellectually and coming face to face with the eventuality as she was doing now were two entirely different matters. It terrified her to think of a world in which Cappy did not exist. She couldn't stand the thought. She wanted to cry out against it with all her strength, and yet she had to control her inner agony and not spoil her homecoming for him. After all, how would it make him feel if she spoke these feelings aloud?

Compounding the heaviness in her heart was a great sense of regret that she had neglected him so shamefully the past ten years. While it was true she telephoned often, calling him at least every month or two, she hadn't come to visit the way she should have. Somehow she would make up to him for her selfishness. Forming this resolve as the two of them carried her luggage into the house, she felt better somehow.

"Some coffee would be fine," she replied in answer to Cappy's offer as they came back into the living room after depositing her suitcases in the bedroom that had been hers before she married.

"Got a potful settin' on the stove waitin' for you," he said in a jocular tone, leading the way into the kitchen. "Figured you ain't had a good cup of coffee since you left here the last time."

They sat at the table in the kitchen where she had eaten so many meals with Cappy in the past. His house didn't have a separate dining room. Charlene raised the cup to her lips and drank the bitter, strong coffee. It gave her warmth and strength. The initial shock of seeing Cappy looking so much older had begun to fade away. She was "Charly" once again, surrounded by her grandfather's affection. For the moment she would just push aside all thoughts except the gladness of being with him in the place that had been home for eight years of her life, years that wouldn't have been so happy and secure were it not for him.

"Can't tell you how sorry I was to hear about you and Paul," Cappy said when the subject came around to her separation. He shook his head slowly to emphasize his regret. "Any chance of patching things up?"

The question was one Charlene had expected from him. He wasn't a church-going man, but he had old-fashioned ideas about marriage: A man and a woman were married in the eyes of God and should remain married until one of them died.

"I really can't say at this point, Cappy," she said honestly. "Paul has been involved with Susan for about six months now, it turns out. She's a young engineer with his firm, just a couple of years out of college—and really nice, too. I met her when she was first hired and liked her. I guess she and Paul were thrown together quite a bit in their work, and . . . you know how these things happen."

Charlene could see that Cappy was taken aback by her matter-of-fact tone. When she first began the explanation, he had looked startled and by the time she had finished, he was subjecting her to a hard scrutiny, as though trying to determine what her real feelings were. Probably he had expected her to be shattered by the desertion of her husband, or at least more upset than she appeared and sounded.

"I don't blame everything on Paul or Susan, either," she continued, finding it strange to have to explain modern-day situations to someone much older than herself. But then Cappy didn't exactly live in the mainstream of American society. "Marriages don't seem to last anymore. You know how much Paul and I have moved around the last ten years—the longest we lived in any one city without moving was three years. You can just imagine how many women I've known during that time, and I can tell you—three-quarters of them were either on their second or third marriage when I met them or else they have been divorced since then."

Charlene thought it best not to get into the reasons for her own marriage's failure, not now anyway. It wasn't a simple matter to explain why two people drift apart and lose their closeness, as she and Paul had done. While there was no doubt that they had been attracted to each other at first and had enjoyed the novelty of marriage for the first two or three years, she wondered deep down if they had ever been deeply and passionately in love. Her decision to marry him had admittedly been influenced by her head as well as her heart.

Cappy was frowning, apparently mulling over Charlene's comments about modern marriages.

"Don't see any reason marriage should be any different now than it ever was," he said firmly, giving an emphatic little nod. "Maybe people don't work at it as hard as they used to. First trouble that comes along they throw up their hands and give up."

Charlene had no desire to argue with him, and she knew Cappy enjoyed nothing more than a good discussion. The subject was far too complex to get into now when she was a little tired from driving and not entirely clear in her thinking at this particular juncture in her life.

"To answer your question about the chance that Paul and I might get back together again, I really don't know," she said thoughtfully. "If he does change his mind and wants to try again, I'll certainly be open on the subject." Her tone indicated that she would rather say nothing more for the time being. Casting around for another topic to introduce, she remembered the work crew she had seen in the section of the marina nearest the entrance. Now it was her turn to frown and to question him.

"What's going on up at the front of the marina anyway? It looks like you're rebuilding the whole place from top to bottom." The note of accusation crept in despite her efforts to sound merely interested.

Cappy got up and went over to the stove to reheat the coffee. His back was turned toward her when he answered.

"Dad-burned insurance company wouldn't renew my policy," he said in a disgusted voice. "Said the pilings wouldn't hold if we had a real wing-dinger of a hurricane come through here." He brought the pot over to the table and refilled both their cups. Then he put the pot back on the stove. "Course they're right," he admitted with a grin, coming back to sit down again at the table. "I figured there was no point in doing the whole thing piecemeal, and I ain't really able to do the work myself. Reckon I'll be forced to raise the slip rent now. That's sure to cause me some problems. Some of these folks—like old man Burns and Bubba Robichaux—they been in here so long they think *they* own the place instead of me."

Charlene smiled in response to his low chuckle. Many of the longtime renters were paying the original slip rent they had paid from the beginning, more than twenty years ago. Cappy had his own system for charging people according to where they were from and how long they had been renting from him. Local people invariably got a more favorable deal than those from New Orleans or Baton Rouge.

"But, Cappy, you must be paying a fortune in interest borrowing money from the bank now," she pointed out in a concerned tone.

He was suddenly engrossed in putting the lid on the sugar bowl and shoving the bowl into the precise center of the table between the salt and pepper shakers. It dawned on Charlene that for the first time in her memory he was being evasive.

"You *did* borrow money from the bank," she persisted.

He met her eyes directly then and read the determination in them. "Nope. Didn't have to. Got me a partner now and he put up the money. Now don't ask me his name," Cappy hastened to add, one hand raised as though to stop her from the question she had opened her mouth to ask him. "Part of the partnership deal is for me not to let on to anybody— leastways for the time being—who he is. Gave my word on that, Charly, so don't you be asking me to break it."

She looked at him for a long moment, fighting down the rising sense of frustration. If Cappy had given his word to this unidentified "partner," she might as well not try to get the man's name out of him. In Cappy's own code of behavior, his word meant a great deal to him. Besides, she had to remind herself, the marina belonged to him and he had every right to do with it what he pleased. She certainly had no right to come here after ten years of virtually neglecting her grandfather and to act as if he had to answer to her for his business actions. She had no choice other than to drop the matter for the time being, even though she was definitely uneasy. What if this silent partner took advantage of Cappy and cheated him out of his ownership of the marina? At Cappy's age that would be tragic. It wasn't as though he were young enough to start over in another business and build security for himself.

She pondered Cappy's revelation about a silent partner while she excused herself and went to the bedroom to unpack and change clothes. Twenty minutes later she emerged wearing jeans and a yellow turtleneck sweater, the outfit as casual as anything she owned now. The jeans bore a label that attested to their price tag.

"Cappy?" she called. When no answer was forth-coming, she surmised that he had probably gone out to the store. This time of year, mid-February, there would be little boat traffic on the river, especially on a weekday, but he puttered around in the store and did paperwork in his office, too.

Intending to go and find him, she walked out first onto the porch running along the front of the house. Cappy called it the "gallery." Stopping to lean her hands on the railing, Charlene gazed out at a scene that struck her anew with its bleak beauty. The placid river was dark and glassy, reflecting the opposite shore, whose cypress trees were stark and craggy this time of year. It wouldn't be long now before the pale green, feathery foliage would begin to appear. Growing beneath the cypress trees were fan-shaped palmettos with their razor-sharp blades and pointed tips. Charlene couldn't name the many other varieties of plants growing in the black, fetid mud of the swamp.

At least the swamp was still safe, she reflected moodily, *uninhabited except by wild creatures.* It would be a while before man conquered nature sufficiently to erect a subdivision there.

Straightening with a sigh, she walked along the porch to the steps leading down to the fuel dock. There was no point in standing about wallowing in gloom. Change was inevitable. She was living proof of that truth herself. It was silly for her to expect one little corner of the world to be frozen in time just for the sake of her own private reassurance.

Entering the store from the fuel dock, she found no one about. Before peeking into the office, she looked around her, noting changes here, too. In the past, the large room had looked something like a storage room with cardboard boxes of wares stacked here and there and various snack foods placed none too neatly on shelves. Now there were more shelves and their contents were neatly arranged. The coolers along one wall were obviously new, not the old chest type Cappy had had before, but the kind with glass doors. She could see they were well stocked with beer and soft drinks.

Was Cappy's new partner responsible for the transformation? she wondered as she turned and walked over to the door opening into the office. The sight that met her eyes there was so astounding she gripped the door facing and stared. Cappy's old mahogany desk had always looked as though it were groaning under its load of papers and debris. The surface was a veritable Noah's Ark with samples of everything that had passed through Cappy's fingers for more than twenty years. And now the desk was so bare the scars and stains in the old varnish were in plain sight.

After looking around the office and noticing new filing cabinets whose drawers actually closed all the way, unlike the drawers in the old cabinets that Cappy had bought from some salvage place, Charlene went over and opened a stiff, new ledger lying on the desk top. Cappy had always kept the sketchiest kind of records. *This new partner, whoever he was, at least was forcing Cappy to run the marina more like a business,* she admitted grudgingly.

Leaving the store through the door on the land side, she took a few steps over to the left and discovered Cappy's whereabouts. He was standing by watching as his fuel tanks were being filled, carrying on a shouted conversation with the driver of the truck. Charlene smiled when Cappy glanced over her way and she made a motion to indicate that she was going to take a walk around the marina.

Intending to avoid the section where the renovation work was in progress, she strolled along the shell-covered road, looking idly at the boats and recognizing some of them as having been there when she first came to live with Cappy. After a while she passed the covered slips and came to the open slips for sailboats. One sailboat caught her eye because it was tied up stern to the dock and she could see the name, *Circe,* and the port, Stewart, Florida. Madisonville was too out of the way to get cruising people just passing through. She assumed someone in the area had bought this boat down in Florida and brought it here. Judging from the open hatches and the dark green, jeeplike vehicle parked in front of the slip, the owner of the boat must be aboard. He had probably dropped by the marina to check his boat for leaks.

Not particularly wanting to get involved in a conversation with anyone at the moment, not even with someone she might know slightly, she started to move along. But she wasn't quick enough. A man emerged from the sailboat and stepped out onto the side pier. Without pausing, Charlene gave him a polite smile and nodded as he strode out to the dark green vehicle. Then she stopped, stared at him incredulously and said, *"Burt?* Burt *Landry?"*

Chapter Two

"How are you, Charly? It's been a while, hasn't it?" he replied easily, his gaze skimming over her and taking note of the sleek cap of black hair she had been wearing long the last time he had seen her, the loose-woven turtleneck sweater and designer jeans, the glove-soft leather shoes with wedge heels.

"Eleven or twelve years, anyway," she murmured, conscious of his open inspection. He was so *different* from the way she remembered him though he really hadn't changed that much. He hadn't put on weight. His medium-height frame was still rangy, almost raw-boned. His hair was still a light brown and his eyes a bright shade of blue.

Suddenly she thought she might have put her finger on the elusive difference in his appearance.

Like so many local boys at that time, Burt had affected the cowboy look. He had worn his hair long with sideburns. It had always looked carefully combed whereas now it was short, and showed no evidence of having been combed at all except by his fingers. He wore old jeans and a plaid flannel shirt, neither with designer labels and neither western-style.

A quizzical gleam in the blue eyes regarding her calmly made Charlene realize how long she had been standing there subjecting Burt to her hard scrutiny. It also occurred to her that he wasn't nearly so surprised at seeing her as she was at running into him. The reason was immediately apparent. He had been forewarned and *she* had not.

"Cappy didn't say a *thing* about your being back in Madisonville!" she exclaimed indignantly. "Is this your sailboat?" she added with a quick change of tone, gesturing toward the boat in question. Her mind was racing now that she had begun to recover from her initial shock at encountering him so unexpectedly. Was Burt also remembering the circumstances under which they had parted? Damn Cappy! Why hadn't he warned her Burt Landry was back in the marina?

"She's mine," he confirmed and let his gaze rove fondly over the boat in that possessive way of owners before he turned his attention to Charlene again. "What time did you arrive?" he asked politely, his tone indicating no genuine interest, but no hint of rancor either. She might have been someone he had known slightly more than a decade ago and was neither particularly pleased nor displeased to encounter again.

Charlene relaxed, relieved that Burt apparently bore her no ill will.

"About an hour and a half ago," she replied, slipping the tips of her manicured fingers into the front pockets of her jeans, which fit too snugly to allow for more than that. "What about you? How long have you been back in Madisonville?" Her own tone, in contrast to his, was genuinely curious. She wondered again why Cappy hadn't mentioned Burt's presence in Madisonville. Cappy and Burt had always been close. From the time Burt was a boy up until he left Madisonville, he had always spent every spare minute around the marina, willing to do anything in the world Cappy asked him to do.

"Oh, a few weeks," he said casually.

"Are you back for good or just visiting your family?" She pressed him.

"Just a visit," he said quickly, folding his arms across his chest and rocking back and forth a little on both feet, which were clad in rubber-soled, brown leather moccasins that had obviously seen much wear. "I'm staying aboard the boat."

Charlene registered the implications of that statement. If Burt were living right here in the marina, she would undoubtedly be running into him often.

"That must really suit Cappy," she remarked, her brown eyes gleaming with a reflective light as she was struck by a sudden thought. Was Burt Landry

Cappy's "silent partner"? She quickly dismissed the notion as being highly improbable. Cappy had said his new partner was putting up the money for the improvements in the marina. Burt's sailboat was beautifully maintained, its hull and decks gleaming with fresh paint, but it wasn't large, perhaps thirty-five feet or so, and it was constructed of wood rather than fiberglass like the expensive, modern yachts. No, she didn't think Burt was the partner. He carried himself with assurance now, the old youthful bluster gone, but he didn't dress like a successful man, and that Volkswagen vehicle parked in front of his slip wasn't a prestige automobile.

A gust of wind pierced the loose weave of Charlene's sweater, and she shivered, hunching her shoulders up against the chill.

"Guess I'd better keep walking," she said, realizing that Burt was just standing there out of politeness anyway. He probably had been on his way somewhere when he stepped out onto the pier and saw her. "It's not quite spring yet, is it? Well, Burt, nice to see you again. I'm sure we'll be running into each other."

His hesitation was fractional. For just a split second, he didn't move or make any response to her pleasant smile. Then he invited in a genial tone, "If you're not in a big hurry, how about a cup of something hot?" The sweep of his arm toward the cockpit of his boat was a deliberately exaggerated gesture of hospitality.

Charlene's hesitation in accepting the invitation

was no longer than his had been in extending it. If Burt were staying in the marina, she undoubtedly would encounter him frequently. So far he hadn't revealed a hint of resentment for her blunt rejection of his overtures twelve years ago. She certainly had no hard feelings against him. If he wanted to be friends now and forget about the past, that was altogether agreeable to her.

"All right," she said and followed along behind him as he walked easily back to the dock and along the side pier.

"Need a hand?" he queried, turning to see her uncertain expression after he had stepped onto the deck.

"I was wondering if these shoes are all right." She stood on one foot, the other one lifted so that the sole of her shoe was visible. "It's some kind of plastic synthetic stuff. I don't think it'll scratch your deck."

"It'll be fine. Just watch your step," he cautioned, holding out a hand to help her aboard.

She took it, feeling the strength of his fingers as they tightened to give her a steadying support. His skin was tough and hard, the skin of a man who worked with his hands. She thought of Paul's hands, as smooth and well-cared for as her own. But then the closest Paul had ever come to manual labor was swinging a golf club or a tennis racquet.

As soon as she had stepped down into the cockpit well, Burt released her hand, not quickly as though the touch of her flesh had bothered him and not reluctantly as though he wished he could prolong the contact. He had simply been helping her aboard his boat and nothing more.

With the agile movements of practice, he preceded her down the companionway ladder. She descended far more slowly, holding on to the sides of the ladder and placing each foot carefully before lifting the other.

"Guess this takes practice," she joked lightly, assuming that he was standing behind her and watching. Most of the men she knew would have made some suggestive and flattering remark about the view of her anatomy she was presenting in the tight jeans. They might even have taken advantage of her situation and rendered aid, grasping her by the waist and setting her on the floor. But Burt did neither. When she reached the bottom of the ladder and turned around, she saw that she had descended into the galley area. He was standing quite close to her, but he was only waiting for her to move past him and get out of his way.

She took several steps and sat down on a settee, looking around her appreciatively. The interior of the boat wasn't large, but it was cozy and attractive, the woodwork trim varnished and the overhead and bulkheads painted a smooth cream color. The upholstery on the cushions was a soft greenish gray, the texture of the material similar to canvas but not as stiff.

"This is very nice," she approved.

"Thanks," he said, his back to her as he rummaged in a locker behind the two-burner stove. "Do you like spiced tea? I have some Red Zinger, which is kind of interesting." He looked over his shoulder at her inquiringly, a wry smile on his lips. "I'm assuming Cappy has already poured some of his coffee down you."

Charlene found it easy to smile back at him. "That's an accurate assumption. I do like spiced tea. I haven't tried Red Zinger, but it sounds too exotic to refuse."

She watched him as he ran water into a kettle, using a hand pump beside the spout. "No pressure water," he volunteered in answer to her unspoken question.

Lighting the burner involved a complex little procedure, she discovered. First he squirted a small amount of liquid from a plastic bottle somewhere down inside the stove and lighted the liquid. After it had flamed brightly for several seconds, he twisted one of the knobs on the front of the stove, and the burner produced a steady blue circle of flame. After setting the kettle in place over the lighted burner, Burt swiveled around and caught the bemused expression on Charlene's face.

"That looks pretty complicated," she said lightly. "Can a mere woman master it?"

"It's not complicated really," he denied, moving over to sit on the settee on the opposite side of the cabin. He leaned back against the bulkhead and extended his legs along the length of the cushion, appearing totally relaxed and in his element. "Your question surprises me. Aren't you a liberated woman?"

She immediately perceived the ironic humor in that question.

"More liberated than I care to be at the moment," she said dryly. "Surely Cappy told you? Two weeks ago my husband moved out of our house into his girl friend's apartment."

The blunt revelation spoken in a matter-of-fact tone brought to his face the same kind of startled attention she had seen on Cappy's face earlier when she had spoken of the same subject. The blue of Burt's eyes was vivid in the subdued lighting of the boat cabin as he studied her features in silence for several seconds.

"He told me you were separated." He hesitated before adding, "You seem to be taking it well."

"I'm hoping the situation is temporary," she admitted and then looked over at the kettle in surprise. Already it had begun to emit a hissing sound.

"Say, that stove of yours is fast once you get it going," she commented. She wasn't trying to change the subject, but as soon as she had spoken she could tell by the expression on his face that *he* thought she was.

"Kerosene produces a very hot flame," he said, rising and going over to the galley area where he got two mugs out of a cupboard and dangled a tea bag into each of them. Then he came back to where she was sitting and opened out the leaves of the table positioned between the two settees. Next he put a pint jar of honey, two paper napkins, and two teaspoons on the table.

All his movements were economical and sure. He betrayed no hint of masculine sheepishness to indicate that he found it strange that he, a man, was waiting on her, a woman, when the traditional pattern was just the opposite. His obvious familiarity with the galley in no way diminished his maleness in Charlene's eyes, if anything quite the contrary. She found herself reflecting that she found him attractive even though he was sending out no vibes that he was even aware of her as a woman.

Was it just feminine perverseness that caused his aloofness to pique her? Twelve years ago he hadn't been able to take his eyes off her if she happened to be in the same room. He had begged her repeatedly to go out with him and showered her with awkward compliments. At the time she had considered his attentions to be nothing more than an unwanted complication in her life.

Apparently silence didn't bother him. He didn't find it necessary to keep the conversation going while he poured boiling water into the two mugs and brought them over to the table. He had already sat down when he half-rose, his eyebrows elevated in question.

"I have sugar if you prefer."

"Oh, no," she demurred. "Honey is fine." She unscrewed the lid and dipped her teaspoon into the thick amber substance. "Actually I don't usually allow myself anything except saccharin. This is a treat."

It was a perfect opening for some kind of compliment on her figure, either direct or subtle, but he made no use of the opportunity. For several moments he was engrossed in spooning a generous amount of honey into his steaming mug, stirring the contents thoroughly and then removing the tea bag and placing it on one of the paper napkins.

Charlene followed his example and then took an experimental sip of her tea. "Hm-m-m. This *is* different." She took another sip. "I think I like it. It has a minty taste, doesn't it?"

He sat back again, swinging both legs up on the settee, one hand loosely clasping the mug.

"Glad you like it," he said pleasantly.

The hot tea warmed Charlene's insides, and she decided to follow Burt's example and make herself comfortable. After rearranging the throw pillow behind her back, she lounged back with a sigh of well-being.

"Tell me what you've been doing all these years," she urged. "I know from Cappy that you've been to lots of places around the world. Madisonville must seem awfully dull to you now."

"I guess it has been quite a few years," he said reflectively, "but they sure didn't seem long when they were going by."

"Believe me, I know what you mean!" Charlene put in feelingly. "It's hard for me to believe I'm really thirty years old. I don't *feel* any older. Before I know it, I'll be forty and saying the same thing." She grimaced distastefully, finding the conversation disquieting. "So tell me some of the exotic places you've seen. I've lived in exciting places like Atlanta and Houston myself," she said in a self-mocking tone.

Burt looked at her over the rim of his mug as he took a gulp of tea.

"When I left here, I went down to Fort Lauderdale, which is—as you probably know—a kind of winter yachting mecca. I got a deckhand job on a 95-foot motor-sailer and spent that winter down in the Caribbean. The guy who owned the boat lived up in Newport. He'd come down for a week or two at a time with his wife and usually with some of their friends, too. Real nice guy.

"In the summer the crew would usually take the boat up on the East Coast. One year we took her to the Med, which was really great. We cruised the coast of Spain and the French and Italian Riviera. Spent several months in the Greek Islands. Court would fly over and meet us at various ports."

"God, that sounds glamorous!" Charlene exclaimed, genuinely enthralled with the glimpse he was giving her of an entirely different world from her own. "How long did you work at this job—and why on earth would you ever quit?"

He shrugged.

"Anything can get old after a while."

Charlene's eyes slid away from the cynical light in his. Was he making a subtle reference to her failed marriage?

"I suppose that's true," she said uncomfortably.

"To answer your question, I crewed on *Mystic Lady* for about four years. After that I bought *Circe* here and fixed her up. She was in pretty bad shape."

Charlene watched in fascination as he stroked his fingers along the smooth varnish of the cabinetry behind the settee on which he was sitting. It was incredibly sensual to see the gentleness of those fingers whose roughened skin and strength she had felt for herself when he helped her aboard earlier. He spoke of his boat almost as if it were a human being—a woman.

"You must have had to work," she suggested tentatively, doing a mental computation. Four years from twelve left eight years he hadn't accounted for. Surely he hadn't been able to live that long off of savings accumulated from a yacht crewman's salary.

A little smile hovering around Burt's lips and the awareness gleaming in his blue eyes made Charlene suspect he had followed her mental processes and was amused. Once again she was on the verge of feeling ill at ease. Was he remembering what she had declared in youthful arrogance twelve years ago? *You'll never amount to anything, Burt Landry! You're just like all the rest of these Madisonville boys!* Charlene cringed at the memory of how she had gone on and on in her anger, making it clear to Burt that she definitely wanted a lot more from life than his father had been able to give his mother: an ordinary frame house, a bunch of kids, and hard work.

"Not a single one of those rich heiresses who came aboard *Mystic Lady* ever seemed taken with the idea of supporting me," he said lazily. "You're right. I had to work. Fortunately, there's plenty of boatyard work in Florida. No need for anybody who can handle a sander or a paintbrush ever to starve."

Something in his tone made her suspect he was enjoying a private joke, but she didn't have an opportunity to dwell on the suspicion.

"What have *you* been doing all these years?" he prompted, echoing her own words.

She shook her head, lips curved in a self-deprecating smile. "Darn, I wish I'd gone first. After hearing about your travels around the world, my life seems terribly suburban and dull." She cocked her head thoughtfully to one side. "Let's see. I've become an expert at moving. Paul and I have moved from Atlanta to Tulsa to Houston and back to Atlanta in ten years. I can pack, settle into a new house, and have a whole new set of friends in a month," she declared with exaggerated boastfulness.

She wished he would smile with her, but he didn't. He just sat quietly waiting for her to continue. Charlene knew that her life-style would probably seem frivolous to him, but then he hadn't exactly been directing the Peace Corps himself. His life seemed totally selfish to her. At least she had created an attractive home for her husband, and had always done her part in furthering his career, entertaining business associates and being the charming wife at company parties and conferences. Bolstered by this reflection, she continued.

"Every time we moved, I usually had to do a

certain amount of redecorating. That's more work and more time-consuming than you realize if you haven't done it, but I enjoyed it thoroughly. It was such a challenge. I even took some interior decorating courses here and there.

"Aside from that and the usual routine of keeping up a house and doing all the shopping and everything, I play quite a bit of tennis and some bridge and take an exercise class. With a bunch of women, there's always shopping and luncheons, too. *Lots* of luncheons!" she proclaimed gaily, determined to inject some light-hearted humor into the situation. The most she got from Burt for her trouble was a smile that was nothing more than cooperation on his part. He wasn't amused, and he had no sympathy for the life-style she was describing to him. On the other hand, she couldn't imagine living cooped up in a little boat like this, either.

"Paul and I are both on the sociable side and like to be around people a lot," she continued. "We do—or *did*, I guess I should say—quite a bit of entertaining, friends as well as his business associates. Entertaining involves a lot of planning and work. It's so hard to keep coming up with a menu that's different and yet not too much involved . . ."

She stopped, astounded at herself and irritated to hear the defensive note in her voice. Why should she defend her activities of the last ten years to Burt Landry? What did it matter whether he approved of her or not?

"You may remember how involved in extracurricular activities I was in school," she said lightly.

"Once a cheerleader, always a cheerleader, I suppose. If there's a committee anywhere around in a fifty-mile radius, I seem to end up on it, more than likely as chairman. But I enjoy being busy and I have to have people around me. Otherwise I'd die of boredom."

Toward the last his eyes had narrowed in response to the hint of belligerence in her tone. He hadn't said a word since she began telling him about her life, not a single word, and yet she had been made to feel defensive.

"You haven't had any children."

It was a statement, not a question. He would know from Cappy that she hadn't. Apparently he wondered why, a curiosity she could understand under the circumstances. Her life was conventional in all other ways.

"No, we haven't been able to have children."

Charlene automatically injected the note of regret in her tone. People expected it, she had learned. While it was true she had always assumed she would have children, the fact that she hadn't so far had not caused her deep grief. It wasn't as though she yearned to be a mother. There wasn't a great gap in her life that only a child could fill. As she had just told Burt, she kept very busy.

"I haven't done anything to prevent pregnancy in the last five years," she explained. "It's my fault I can't get pregnant. My uterus is turned the wrong way. Paul and I weren't in favor of adopting. I suppose it's pretty egotistical, but we wanted a baby that was *us*."

"I would have thought—what with all the advances in medical science—" He broke off, his expression indicating a realization that what he had been about to say was none of his business.

He didn't have to finish the conjecture. It was common knowledge that many with Charlene's problem went to doctors who were working with methods of implanting a husband's sperm into the wife's uterus. One of the doctors she had seen had suggested she investigate the possibility. He had even given her the name of a clinic in Tulsa, where she had been living at the time. But Paul had been transferred again, this time to Houston, and in all the bustle of moving again, she had pushed the matter out of her mind. Since then she'd never gotten around to pursuing it further.

"I guess things all work out for the best," she theorized philosophically, ready to drop the subject of her childlessness. "If Paul and I get a divorce, at least there won't be a custody problem."

"If?"

Charlene met the inquiry in his gaze candidly.

"Susan, the girl Paul's fallen madly in love with, is twenty-three. That's nine years' difference in age. Plus she'd bright and ambitious, the career woman all the way. Frankly I don't think their infatuation will last. Paul's and mine didn't," she added honestly. "Marriage is a practical, convenient living arrangement, not some sublime existence up on a cloud. I was very satisfied with my marriage. I liked my life as Paul's wife. If he gets over this little fling, I'd seriously consider taking him back."

Charlene was taken aback by her own forthrightness, never before having expressed her pragmatic views on marriage quite this openly. They had evolved through the years of her own marriage and were based on close observation of the social institution so integral to western society. Perhaps Burt's remoteness from her way of life enabled her to speak so bluntly. Suddenly she realized she had only been assuming he was unmarried himself. She hadn't asked him.

"I haven't even asked you about your marital status," she said, looking at his ringless left hand lying on the table.

"How many women would find the way I live a 'practical, convenient living arrangement'?" he asked cynically. "The popular myth has always been that women are the romantic ones, but they aren't, are they? It's men who are searching for that elusive thing called love, and they end up being taken every time. What they thought was starlight in those adoring female eyes was pure calculation." His reflective tone was heavily laced with irony.

Charlene had to acknowledge that she had left herself wide open for that unflattering analysis of her sex. Even as she made her defense, she had to wonder how many times Burt had pursued love with a woman and been "taken." Judging from his manner with herself, he didn't trust women and didn't waste any time or energy playing the usual man-woman games, which even married men and women slipped into automatically.

"I don't agree with you at all," she declared

strongly. "Men don't get 'taken' any more than women do. It's just that the initial attraction between a man and a woman doesn't last. The relationship changes as a couple becomes more familiar with each other. That's all I meant. And even though the man is the provider in the traditional marriage, the woman does her share, too, even if she doesn't always earn money."

Hearing the vehemence in her voice, Charlene knew it was stronger than it should be. She sounded as if she might be trying to convince herself as well as him, and this man across from her was far too perceptive to be unaware of that fact. Aside from the color of his hair and eyes, the shape of his features, and his general physical build, she'd discovered there was little resemblance between him now and the youth who had tried to mask his insecurity with cockiness twelve years ago. The blue eyes held a glint of cynical humor, a worldweariness. He had seen much of the world outside the confines of Madisonville, and his expression said he wasn't easily impressed. She wondered if he wasn't asking himself what he had ever seen in *her*.

"Well, thanks for the tea," she said a little abruptly, glancing toward the open hatch and seeing that the light outside seemed to have grown dimmer. "Guess I'd better get back to the house. Cappy will be wondering what happened to me." She got up and moved toward the companionway ladder. Going up was much easier than backing down it had been.

Burt followed her out and stood in the cockpit while she stepped out onto the side pier, managing to do so without any assistance. Some difference in the marina claimed her attention, and she realized it was quiet now. The hum of the machinery had ceased. Evidently the work crew had gone home.

For a while down in Burt's boat, she had forgotten all about the construction. Her face saddened as she thought about it now and about other changes that were even more distressing.

"Cappy's finally getting old, Burt," she said bleakly, her dark eyes filled with pain as they met his.

He didn't offer her any easy reassurances. Nodding his head in agreement, he said, "It's going to happen to all of us, Charly, if we're lucky. Cappy's had a good life. He *still* has a good life. I don't know anyone any happier."

She felt strangely comforted by the quiet words and bonded to him by their mutual affection for Cappy. That use of her old nickname had come so naturally to his lips. Human empathy flowed between them, making the moment an intimate one.

It occurred to her that Burt might know something about the partnership to which Cappy had referred to so vaguely. A little frown creased her forehead as she wondered how best to approach the matter and decided not to be direct.

"I wish Cappy had talked to me before he went into partnership with somebody," she said in a worried tone. "You don't suppose he's being taken advantage of, do you?"

Burt's expression betrayed no emotion except lack of concern. He either didn't know any more than she did or else he considered the partner trustworthy.

"I think Cappy's too smart to let anybody take advantage of him. I wouldn't worry about it if I were you," he advised.

"You're probably right," she agreed. "Well, thanks again for the tea. I guess I'll probably be seeing you around."

"Sure thing."

A quick look over her shoulder when she had started on her way back out toward the river showed that Burt wasn't standing and watching her go. He had already gone down inside the boat.

She just couldn't get over the change in him! There was nothing of the small-town boy about him now. His speech, his movements, his manner all had about them a casual assurance that made the word *sophistication* come to mind, in spite of the way he lived and the total lack of concern for showiness in his dress and his choice of vehicle.

It had been years since she had thought of Burt. During those first years after he had left Madisonville, Cappy would mention having heard from him every now and then. She didn't know how much Cappy knew or guessed about what had taken place between herself and Burt prior to his leaving. Certainly she had never mentioned to Cappy that ghastly scene that had been a kind of inevitable culmination of circumstances.

Even as she remembered the confrontation she was filled with warring emotions. How much of it had been her fault after all? Had she encouraged Burt to think he might have a chance to win her? She didn't think she had, but then she had been an awful flirt back in those days, riding high on the cloud of high-school popularity. It had seemed her due that every young male she encountered should eye her with admiration and longing, as most of them did. She just hadn't stopped to think that Burt was older than the boys at school. The year he suddenly started paying her so much attention she had been a senior in high school, which would have meant he was twenty-one—a man, not a boy—and holding down a full-time job.

Before that year he had always been a familiar figure around the marina, and he had teased her good-naturedly, but she knew he was there because of Cappy, not her. He adored Cappy and would do anything for him. Apparently he never tired of hearing the older man's yarns of his days as a tugboat captain. The first time he asked her to go out with him, she had been shocked and had, of course, refused, but with a teasing excuse that would allow him to think she would *like* to go but had too many other obligations. In her own mind, it was her way of not hurting his feelings.

At that time she was one of the most popular girls at Mandeville High School, a member of the "in" crowd, which meant her closest friends were country club kids who lived in the affluent subdivisions in the area. She went to parties and spent the night with girl friends whose parents all drove their own Mercedes. The boys she dated would go to college and become professional men or executives. The mothers of her friends were attractive, charming women who wore beautiful clothes and spent much of their time playing tennis or golf and going to luncheons while still managing, with the help of their maids, to maintain huge, gorgeous houses. Charlene knew she wanted to live that kind of life herself, a life where one was insulated by wealth and privilege. Nothing unpleasant, certainly nothing tragic, seemed possible in a world like that.

A local Madisonville boy like Burt Landry, no matter how nice he was or how attractive, couldn't possible have fit into the future she envisioned for herself. His family were respectable, hard-working people, his father a foreman at the shipyard outside of town, his mother a plump, domestic woman whose center of existence was her home and family. The Landrys didn't owe a penny on their house, but it was just a plain, wood-frame house, typical of those in the area, a vegetable garden out back and the neatly mowed lawn showing no touch of the professional landscaper's hand.

In short, while there was nothing *wrong* about Burt or his family, Charlene could see that he would turn out just like his father, and the woman he eventually married would need to be essentially like his mother, devoted to the physical well-being of her husband and children. As soon as Burt had graduated from high school, he had immediately taken a job as a welder in the shipyard, where presumably he would stay, with little chance of ever advancing any higher than his father had. It would have been pointless for her to date Burt since she wanted more from life than he would ever be able to give her, but she hadn't wanted to tell him that. She hadn't wanted to hurt his feelings.

Then during the Christmas holidays she had met Paul Reed at a party, and he had all the qualifications Burt lacked. Paul's father was a high-ranking executive for an oil company. His mother was the essence of the kind of woman Charlene hoped to be someday, stylish and poised and charming. The Reeds lived in a beautiful house and seemed to enjoy the best that life had to offer. Paul himself, a sophomore at LSU, was attractive in a quiet, bookish kind of way and a better-than-average student in school. After two dates, Charlene "set her cap" for him. He wasn't Robert Redford, but he was considerate and courteous, he seemed to adore Charlene from the first, and not least in importance—he offered her an *entrée* into the kind of life she wanted for herself.

Those last few months of high school had been hectic ones and edged with poignancy as she felt herself poised on the threshold of the adult world. Leaving high school seemed tantamount to leaving childhood behind. Charlene often felt herself on the verge of tears for no reason at all. She was in such a mood one night when she walked outside the gym following a particularly grueling rehearsal of the children's play in which she played one of the leads. There waiting for her in his pickup truck was Burt Landry. Without any forewarning of his intentions, he had decided to come for her and give her a ride home.

It was the worst possible move he could have made. He looked ludicrously "wrong" in her school habitat with his sideburns and western-style clothes. She had heard a muffled giggle and someone had whispered, "Who's Charly's redneck friend?"

Rather than make a scene, she had climbed into Burt's truck, a shiny new red one that was his pride and joy. But on the ride home, she had been unable to hide her irritation, answering all his questions in a clipped, icy tone. By the time they got to the marina, the atmosphere in the truck's cab was tense and Burt had stopped trying to make conversation with her.

"I know what's wrong with you!" he had burst out angrily as he brought the pickup to a jolting halt outside of Cappy's house. "You think you're too good for me, don't you? You with all your country club friends. Well, don't worry. You won't be bothered with me again."

Later Charlene wished she had just gotten out of the pickup and gone inside, but several incidents had occurred that day to wear on her nerves, and she was tired. Before she could stop herself, she was blazing back at him.

"I wish you *would* stop pestering me, Burt Landry! I've tried to tell you in a nice kind of way I don't *want* to go out with you! You're not my type!"

"And just what *is* your type?" he had snarled back.

Charlene always cringed when she recalled her next words. She couldn't explain exactly what had happened, but some restraint inside her had snapped and she had heard herself telling Burt the bald truth.

"It's certainly not somebody from Madisonville!" she had hissed sarcastically. "Not somebody who's going to work in a shipyard his whole life and not amount to anything! I want to live in a nice place like Beau Chene or Country Club Estates in a big house. I want pretty clothes and my own fancy little car—" She broke off, the tears she had been holding back all day spilling down her cheeks and muffling her voice.

"I'm sorry, Burt. I didn't mean to hurt your feelings. Honest. But I don't understand guys like you. Don't you have any ambition? Don't you want to *be* somebody? The way you're going you'll be just like your father. Look how many years he worked in that shipyard just to be a foreman, and that's as far as he can go. You have to have a college degree to get anywhere in this world today. Why didn't you go to college? You're smart enough." Her voice had lost all its earlier vehemence and was filled with a blend of apology and pleading. But she could tell by his face and the expression in his eyes that she had wounded his feelings deeply.

"I'm smart enough where you're concerned," he said bitterly. "You've got dollar signs in those pretty brown eyes of yours. I pity the poor bastard that gets you. He might never know it, but it won't be *him* you're interested in, but what he can give you—"

"I don't have to listen to any more of this!" Charlene had cried out furiously, jerking open the door of the truck. She had run into the house, thoroughly shaken by the whole ugly encounter and wishing it had never happened. She knew Burt had spoken with the intention of hurting her as she had hurt him, but his words stirred a deep uneasiness inside her, and she found herself trying to refute the accusation that she was heartless and mercenary, as he had made her sound.

She wasn't! She had emotions and feelings like everyone else, but she also wanted certain things out of life. Common sense told her she would have to marry a man with a future. Damn it! The last thing she wanted to do was hurt Burt like that! His vulnerability had quivered like an exposed, naked creature for several seconds until he had covered his feelings with anger. There had been raw anguish in his tone as well as hate and fury when he attacked her.

She hadn't seen him again after that, not until today. Two weeks after their bitter exchange he had quit his job and left Madisonville. She learned the news from Cappy one night when she came home from school after some evening function. Burt had come by the marina to tell Cappy good-bye. He was heading down to Florida. While he was still young and not tied down, he wanted to see something of the world.

Charlene hadn't said anything to Cappy about the guilt she felt at Burt's leaving. Deep down she had always thought *she* was responsible for his actions, coming as they did so soon after the ugly confrontation with him. Eventually, though, she had forgotten about him, pushing the whole experience to the back of her mind along with the doubts about herself that Burt had provoked with his hurtful accusations.

"Why didn't you mention that Burt Landry was living here in the marina?" she asked Cappy as soon as she got back to the house. He had already locked up the store and was watching television, an episode of the old "I Love Lucy" show he doubtlessly had seen many times before, but he never tired of the series.

His attention was concentrated on the screen for a few seconds longer, and he chuckled aloud, slapping his knee. "That crazy woman!" he exclaimed and then looked around at Charlene, who had sat on the sofa. "What was that you said?"

"I ran into Burt Landry. He told me he's living aboard his boat here in the marina. I wondered why you hadn't mentioned it to me."

Cappy's mild surprise seemed genuine.

"Guess I didn't think of it. He looks good, don't he?"

Charlene agreed and then turned her gaze to the television screen as if she, too, were watching the program. By the time the next commercial flashed on, she had decided how to phrase the question she wanted to ask.

"Cappy, wasn't it kind of sudden the way Burt left Madisonville? I remember wondering at the time if something had happened with his family or his job." There. She was giving Cappy a wide-open range for telling her *she* had been the cause of Burt's leaving.

After all, it had all happened twelve years ago. She and Burt were different people by now. Why not bring everything out into the open?

Cappy struck a match and held it to his pipe. His cheeks sucked in as he drew deeply on it, making the tobacco glow red.

"In a way it was kind of sudden, I reckon. I think he saw that the longer he put off leaving, the harder it would be for his folks. He tried to tell his pa when he took that job welding in the shipyard that it wasn't what he wanted to do all his life. He didn't know what that was, but he figured he'd work in the shipyard and save his money in the meantime. We even talked about him and me becoming partners one of these days."

Cappy took several draws on his pipe, sending out aromatic clouds of smoke. Charlene digested what he had just told her with some surprise. She hadn't known Burt didn't intend to work permanently in the shipyard. From Cappy's faintly regretful tone when he mentioned the prospect of a partnership between himself and Burt, she could infer the answer to a question she hadn't gotten around to asking yet. Obviously Burt was not Cappy's present "silent partner."

"I wasn't real surprised when Burt just up and took off like that," Cappy was continuing in a reflective tone. "He had this wanderlust thing in him that had to be satisfied. Don't ask me where he got it from. His mamma and his pa never wanted to go anywhere their whole lives. Doubt either one of 'em's been further than Louisiana and Mississippi. But Burt was always a dreamer. Always reading books about sailing around the world."

Charlene didn't attempt to hide her amazement at this description of Burt. She'd certainly never thought of him as a dreamer nor as the type to read books! To her, he had just been a typical local boy, with little interest in school except perhaps for playing football. High school was a time for getting into minor scrapes, for playing pranks like painting vulgar insults all over the facade of a rival school or stealing road signs and relocating them in inappropriate places. As soon as the typical local boy got his diploma, the time for youth was over. He would marry young and follow in his father's footsteps, going into partnership with him if he had some little business, or taking a job with his company if he happened to work in a shipyard or a plant. Burt had seemed to be following the pattern when he took a job welding in the shipyard where his father was a foreman.

"I Love Lucy" was over. Cappy got up and turned the channel selector and then came back to his chair, settling down to watch the afternoon news.

"That mayor's race in New Orleans is going to be a nasty one," he commented.

Charlene sat quietly and watched the news with him, taking her eyes from the screen frequently and gazing at him lovingly. He was so dear to her, even more so because she perceived him as fragile now. The subject of Burt Landry was forgotten for the time being. Her pleasure in being here with Cappy was poignant and intense. There was no reason she had to be in any hurry to get back to Atlanta. She would stay with Cappy awhile, pamper him and take care of him. Maybe she could make up for the years of selfishness.

Chapter Three

It was hard to believe this was really February and not June, but the weather in south Louisiana was utterly capricious. Charlene could remember more than one Christmas when the temperature had soared up into the seventies. Sprawling a little lower into the aluminum patio chair, she extended her legs straight out in front of her and tipped her head back to get the full benefit of the bright sunshine. She might as well go back to Atlanta with a suntan—

Catching herself in the middle of that idle thought, she sat up straight again, sighing. As much as she hated to admit it, she was restless after only a week. There just wasn't much going on this time of year. On the weekends a few boat owners came to the marina, mostly to check on their boats, but there was little traffic on the river. Come May and June, it would be churned up with water-skiers and Cappy would be busy at the fuel dock and in the store, but now it was quiet, especially on a weekday.

Charlene was used to being busy every second, and she didn't know what to do with all this time on her hands. She had too much time to think, and much of what she had to think about was deeply unsettling. It was beginning to look as if Paul was really serious about getting a divorce. She had been so hopeful that he would get over his little fling and want to come back to her, but it seemed not to be the case. He had telephoned her a couple of evenings ago to get her thoughts on selling the house. Did she have any asking price in mind and was there a particular real estate agency she preferred? He had wanted to know. He thought they should sell the house before having a property settlement.

Underneath his faintly apologetic tone was a finality she found chilling. It looked as if she were really going to find herself a divorced woman, whether she wanted to be or not. Maybe Paul wasn't going to come to his senses as she had expected him to do. Maybe he wasn't going to see that he was making a mistake.

Where did that leave her? What was she going to do? The divorce lawyer she had consulted before leaving Atlanta had assured her she would have no problem in getting substantial alimony, for several years, anyway. Women in her circumstances were usually given a period of time in which to prepare themselves to earn a living.

And the property settlement would leave her with a nice sum of money. She could buy a smaller house or a condominium. But what would her life be like when she no longer had a husband and a secure home? *She would have to start thinking about a job or a career,* she supposed, but the prospect didn't fill her with enthusiasm. She'd never had any desire to be a super career woman.

The throbbing sound of an engine grew louder, drawing her attention over to the right where a boat was motoring out of the marina into the river. It was Burt Landry. Standing in the cockpit of his sailboat, one hand on the tiller and one foot propped up on the seat, he looked casual in faded, cutoff jeans and a tee shirt. Evidently he planned to go out for a sail on Lake Pontchartrain.

Charlene had seen him every day since her arrival, sometimes several times a day since he was in and out of the store to see Cappy for one reason or another, frequently just to chat with him. Burt was always friendly and courteous to Charlene, but he showed absolutely no interest in spending time in her company. She was unused to being treated with such indifference by a male contemporary. In her own social set, she was used to the man-woman repartee that was basically harmless and enjoyable. Burt's politely distant manner made her wonder if perhaps he didn't still hold a grudge against her after all these years.

Now she was stirred by a totally irrational resentment. Here he was on this beautiful, sunny day going out for a sail while she sat on the fuel dock with nothing to do. The least he might have done was ask her if she'd like to go along.

He had come almost abreast of the fuel dock when she was struck by a wild impulse and acted on it immediately. Jumping to her feet, she cupped her hands around her mouth and yelled, "Hey, that's no fair! I want to go too!"

She expected him to smile and wave and yell something back, but instead he headed the boat immediately toward the dock, apparently having taken her seriously.

"You have a nice day for a sail," she said when he had come alongside the dock. To show him that she had only been joking and did not want to foist herself upon him, she sank back down on the plastic webbing of the chair.

His blue eyes squinted a little against the brightness of the sun as he let his gaze run over the bareness of her arms and legs, exposed by the briefness of her white shorts and bright yellow tank top.

"Want to comé along or not?" he asked, reaching over and grasping a massive bronze cleat on the dock to hold the boat off.

His tone of voice indicated to Charlene he wasn't going to wait around all day and cajole her. She had to make up her mind instantly, and one way or the other he would be on his way.

"Sure you don't mind company?" she asked, wanting to be reassured. "I'd like to go!" she added quickly when he let go of the cleat and straightened, as if intending to motor away from the dock.

"Come aboard then," he instructed, holding out a hand to her.

She had been sitting barefoot and didn't take time now to buckle on her sandals. Instead she picked them up and taking his hand, stepped down onto the deck of the sailboat and from there into the cockpit's well. Exhilaration tilted her mouth into a smile until it occurred to her suddenly that Cappy would wonder what had happened to her.

"Cappy!" she yelled.

He appeared in the open door and waved when he saw her in the boat. Then he disappeared back inside.

"This is great!" she exulted as the crisp breeze lifted her hair. A minute ago she had been bored to death and now she was off on an adventure. "I've always wanted to go sailing!"

"You've never been sailing?"

His eyes flicked over her again, noting but not paying homage to the care she'd taken in keeping her figure trim. A little irked, she sat back with both arms resting behind her on the cockpit coaming, a position that thrust her breasts into prominence.

"No, I never have," she answered. "I've been out in those fast ski boats and once out into the Gulf deep-sea fishing, but never sailing. If you want me to do something, you'll have to tell me."

Her smile and tone were guaranteed to stroke the male ego, but they had no noticeable effect on him. *It wasn't natural for a man to be that impervious to a normally attractive female,* she reflected. Evidently Burt had never forgiven her for her cruel words to him twelve years ago. Incredible as it was to think he could hold a grudge that long, she could think of no other explanation.

Today would be the perfect opportunity for her to smooth his wounded male ego. They would be together out on the lake for hours, and surely proximity would have a healing effect. She would like to be friends with him. It was lonely in the marina and he was somebody close to her own age she could talk to.

When they had motored the two and a half miles down river and passed through the drawbridge, Burt gave her casual instructions: "Here, you sit next to the tiller and steer while I take off the sail covers. Just keep her in the middle of the river."

Charlene carried out her assignment with the greatest trepidation at first. She'd never steered a sailboat before, and it took some experimenting to ascertain that if she wanted to go to the right, she had to push the tiller in the opposite direction. After five minutes or so, she had begun to feel more confident and could allow herself to watch Burt as he moved with easy confidence around the boat, taking off the black sail covers and attaching ropes here and there. When she wasn't watching him, noting with appreciation the supple leanness of his body and his peaceful absorption in his tasks, she looked out at the banks of the river, noting the beginnings of spring greenery.

For a long stretch there was nothing but marshland on either side of the river. Then they came to the small, weathered camps on pilings at the mouth of the river and the huge sheds where people fished off the piers. By this time Burt had completed his preparations, but he didn't take over the tiller when he returned to the cockpit. Secretly Charlene was pleased that he didn't. It made her feel she was doing a competent job of steering the boat.

The water got choppier in the L-shaped channel that took them from the river into the lake. As soon as they turned sharply to the left just in front of the lighthouse, which looked picturesque and lonely on its barren point of land, Burt put up the sails and turned off the engine. A huge vacuum of silence was soon filled with the gurgling of water against the hull and the brushing of wind along the taut sails.

"It's so *quiet*," Charlene remarked in an awed tone.

Burt nodded in agreement, settling down in the cockpit and taking over the tiller.

"I've never understood the attraction of power boats. It's too much like driving a car to me," he said thoughtfully.

"This is nice. I like it," she declared, relaxing bit by bit as she realized the boat really wasn't going to tip all the way over.

"This breeze is just right, not too strong and not too light. Part of the endless fascination of sailing is that you can never predict exactly what it's going to be like when you go out. So much depends on the conditions of wind and sea."

"Watching you, it all seemed so complicated," she observed, liking the contemplative cast of his features. He seemed so totally in harmony with his surroundings while she still felt a little strange, unaccustomed to the movements of the boat or to its sideways angle.

"It isn't complicated really. In fact, it's quite simple. The terminology tends to put people off at first."

When he didn't volunteer more, she asked him questions, mainly just to keep him talking about the subject in which he was so obviously interested. She liked to watch his face while he talked. Then after a while the conversation dwindled, and both of them seemed content just to think their own thoughts. The rhythmic motion and restful sounds had their effect on Charlene. She felt a sense of deep peacefulness easing its way into her body and taking over her mind, too.

"Want a beer?"

The question startled her into alertness.

"That sounds good," she said, sitting up straight and stretching. "I think I was about to fall asleep on you."

"No *about* to it. You *were* asleep," he accused dryly and grinned at her.

She smiled back, strangely warmed at this show of friendliness. During the short time it took him to go down inside the boat and return with two cold cans of beer, she debated with herself. Should she leave well enough alone or should she ask him point-blank if he still harbored a grudge against her? If he did, she could apologize and ask his forgiveness. It would make her feel better even if it didn't totally obliterate the damage.

When he came out, she saw that he had taken off the tee shirt. His shoulders and arms and chest were smooth and tanned, the growth of hair so fine and light it was hardly discernible. He stood beside Charlene for just a moment as he handed her the beer, and she could smell the warm muskiness of his flesh. The sharp stirring of awareness inside her came as a distinct surprise, but then she didn't know why it should. Burt was definitely an attractive male, and she had all the normal desires of a healthy female.

"Thanks," she said, taking the can and drinking deeply from it at once. The beer was cold and delicious. "Hm-m-m. This sure hits the spot," she said, watching him as he took several gulps from his own can, his throat convulsing with the swallows. He made a sound of pure animal pleasure as he lowered the can. Somehow Charlene was encouraged that he seemed to have lowered his guard in her presence.

"Thanks for letting me come out here with you today," she said warmly. "I know it was pushy of me to invite myself along, but it is pretty boring in the marina."

His gaze collided with hers for a long second and then swung away. He took another deep gulp of his beer before he answered.

"I would have asked you myself if I had thought you would want to go," he said politely, looking up at the sails as if checking to see if they were drawing properly.

Mentally she heaved a sigh. So much for the brief camaraderie between them. He had pushed her away at arm's length again. The only explanation was that he had never forgiven her for what she'd said twelve years ago.

"Would it do any good now if I apologized?" she asked bluntly, hoping to take him by surprise.

The blue eyes flashed with a light that told her she had been successful in startling him, but he looked away before replying. His tone as well as his words were stubbornly uncooperative.

"You don't have to apologize. I'm glad to have the company," he said politely.

"That's not what I meant, and you know it."

She had been lying on the leeward side, her body wedged comfortably between the cockpit coaming and the seat. Now with some effort she sat up, swinging her feet down into the well.

"Burt, why don't we just bring it out into the open and talk about it like adults? You're still holding a grudge against me, aren't you? Well, I can't say that I blame you. The things I said to you that night you came to school and picked me up were truly unforgivable. But that was twelve years ago, for God's sake. I was eighteen years old at the time. Can't we just forget it ever happened? I am truly sorry."

His eyes were riveted upon her face while she talked. When she had finished, he didn't reply at once, his forehead knit into a little frown.

"What have I said or done to make you think—" he began.

"Oh, knock it off!" Charlene interrupted impatiently. "I'm not stupid! You don't act the way a man does with a woman. I don't mean to brag, but I haven't been around too many men who treat me like a sack of flour or—or a post or something!"

The intentness of his regard was making her vaguely ill at ease. She was already beginning to wish she hadn't forced this subject out into the open.

"You're the married granddaughter of a man I dearly love and respect. Surely you didn't expect me to make a pass at you," he said cynically.

Heat surged though Charlene's veins. He was being deliberately obtuse, taking the opportunity to cause her embarrassment and thereby proving her initial suspicion that he still resented her deeply.

"I'm not exactly a teen-ager anymore," she said hotly, "and before long I won't be married. But that's all beside the point. Just forget the whole thing! Keep that chip on your shoulder if you like it there!"

She got up and managed to make her way down the companionway ladder. Inside the boat, she walked forward to the head with little difficulty, finding the movement regular and easy to adjust to. Overhead she could hear noises like the flapping of sails, but she wasn't concerned. However narrow-minded Burt Landry might be, he had impressed her with his competency in handling the boat. Whatever was happening out there was fully under his control, she was sure.

When she came out of the little enclosed head, it dawned on her that something was entirely different. They weren't moving anymore! The boat now seemed to float in the water, completely upright rather than tilted over on its side. Light footsteps sounded overhead and then she heard Burt step down into the cockpit well. Before she could move, his body was blocking out the light from the open hatchway. He was coming down inside the boat.

Charlene stood uncertainly in the middle of the cabin, questioning him with her eyes. "We aren't moving," she said, trying not to sound as uneasy as she felt. "What happened?"

Her heart began beating a staccato rhythm against her breastbone when she saw the way Burt was looking at her. There was nothing impersonal about his lingering survey of her figure now. His blue eyes were stripping away her clothes piece by piece. Surely he didn't *think*— Surely he didn't mean to— Her suspicions were too outlandish even to complete!

"Don't look so scared. Nothing's wrong. I just took down the sails and put out the anchor," Burt reassured softly, taking several languid steps that brought him so close to her she could feel the heat pulsing out from his naked upper torso. Slowly he reached both hands toward her and lightly cupped her shoulders.

"Wh-Why did you take down the sails?" she questioned breathlessly, her gaze imprisoned by the blue intensity of his. This just *couldn't* be happening! Surely Burt hadn't mistaken her words out there for an invitation! If he had, she would have to put him straight.

"Burt, I hope you didn't get the wrong idea— I wasn't implying—that is, I didn't mean—"

He had taken a half step closer so that their bodies

were almost touching. Without increasing his hold on her shoulders, he bent his head and grazed his lips along the bare flesh of her neck. His breath was hot and brought instant prickles. Charlene started involuntarily and then jerked away from him, backing up until her hip rested against the pedestal of the drop-leaf table.

"I don't believe this!" she exclaimed, her voice too high and threaded with a brittle note of hysteria. "I was simply trying to apologize to you for a wrong done twelve years ago! My intention was *not* to seduce you, believe me!"

The expression on Burt's face did not change, nor did his eyes lose their glow of blatant sexuality. Charlene had a sense of panic as he slowly closed the small distance she had put between them. Had he even heard her words?

"You were right out there, Charly," he said softly. "I guess I have been carrying a grudge all these years. And that is pretty silly, under the circumstances. Why don't we just let bygones be bygones? I'm willing if you are."

Charlene stood there unresisting while his arms slid around her rigid form, overwhelmed by a sense of incredulity at what he apparently intended. His soft voice had been like a caressing breeze playing over her flesh, and she fought against its invitation the same way she fought against the weakness that invaded her knees when Burt planted little kisses at the side of her neck, pushing his face up under the sleek curve of her black hair to the sensitized area just behind her ear. She shivered involuntarily.

"Burt, I'm not going to let you make love to me," she declared firmly. "I'd like to be friends with you, but I am still married and we don't really know each other that well . . ."

She hoped he didn't hear the hint of something akin to desperation in her voice warring with the resolution. While she was speaking, his hands had slid lower and were cupping her buttocks, pulling her pelvis against his into an intimate contact that immediately awakened a pleasurable ache she recognized for what it was, pure and simple physical need. She had been apart from Paul for three weeks now, but it had been considerably longer than that since he had last made love to her.

"You don't have to do anything you don't want to do," Burt was murmuring against her neck, taking little tastes of her flesh. "I'd never force you."

She put out her hands, meaning to push against his chest, but the same instant her palms made contact with the warm hardness of his flesh, he murmured those words so devastating to a woman.

"I want you, Charly," he groaned softly, openly admitting his need.

The hands she willed to push against him and end the contact eroding all her will power moved instead with experimental slowness, noting the resiliency of the skin, the hardness underneath, the pounding drum of his heartbeat. Against all her common sense, Charlene explored the smooth contours of his chest and then moved up to caress the bare shoulders and the tense muscles in his neck.

"Burt, *please,*" she said in a voice that held as much longing as reluctance.

He raised his head and looked into her eyes for a long moment, searching for an answer he apparently found because his gaze dropped to her mouth and he lowered his lips to meet hers. Charlene couldn't force herself to stop him with words or to twist her head aside. Everything inside her wanted the kiss. The desire sweeping her body might be wanton, but it was overpowering her qualms.

The kiss was hard and hungry, a total possession that left her weak and helpless. With little provocation her mouth opened to the questing intimacy of his tongue's invasion, and she met and answered its demands. Only when she thought her heart would explode in her chest and her lungs collapse for want of oxygen did he soften the kiss and give both of them a chance to catch their breath, but the effort his restraint cost him was apparent. It was all he could do to maintain control of his unleashed passion. Shudders rippled through his frame as he tightened his arms around her, pulling his lips from hers and burying his face into her neck.

"Charly, I need you," he murmured against her skin. "Let me make love to you."

The plea seemed strange to Charlene, aroused as she was, her body aglow with hundreds of little flames and her blood turned into a molten liquid desire. She wanted Burt to make love to her. The realization was like an electrical shock jolting her brain. She was in the arms of a man who wasn't Paul, who wasn't the husband she had lived with and been faithful to for ten years! Of course, she had flirted with many men during those years and perhaps even fantasized about making love to them, but what was happening to her now was no fantasy. If she didn't stop things now, at once, it would be too late.

"No!" she burst out, twisting out of his arms.

He didn't try to hold her. His arms dropped away and he stood there looking at her, his mouth twisted into a contemptuous mockery of a smile, his blue eyes scornful.

"How foolish of me to be so presumptuous," he said with cutting irony. "Things haven't really changed that much, have they, Charly? You can't bring yourself to make love with an ordinary man, but you have to make every man want you. Still the little tease, aren't you?"

She flinched at the savagery in his tone, which as much as the words themselves told her she had been right in her intuition that he had never forgiven her.

"You're still bitter, aren't you?" she said regretfully, wishing that she had handled things better just now. This second rejection would do nothing to improve his opinion of her, and it was important to her that he realize he was wrong about her—she hadn't meant to lead him on today. She just wanted to be friends.

"Damn right I'm bitter," he said curtly. "How would you have felt if someone you idolized came right out and told you that you weren't good enough for him? I blame myself more than you, though. I always have. It was stupid of me to be such a romantic idiot. I made you into some kind of ideal of feminine grace and beauty and sweetness that doesn't exist on this earth. It came as a low blow to discover you were nothing more than a heartless little flirt." His blue eyes swept her from the silky cap of black hair to the bare feet and then he moved swiftly toward the companionway ladder, obviously having nothing more to say.

Charlene watched him as he climbed the steps with supple sureness, furious with herself that she had bungled matters so badly and filled with regret for her role in making Burt so cynical about women in general. How appalling to know the negative effect she apparently had had upon his life and his relationships with women. Was it her fault he had never married?

He was moving around up on deck now, the clink of chain telling her that he was hauling up the anchor. Then there was the rustle of sails and the slide of metal against metal. He was getting the boat under sail again.

Feeling miserable, Charlene made her way to the companionway and climbed the steps. In the cockpit she sat and waited for Burt to complete his tasks up on the foredeck and come back to take the tiller. When he did, he didn't give her so much as a glance. She might not even have been there as far as he was concerned.

When she looked to determine their direction, she wasn't surprised to see that they were headed back toward the channel. The lighthouse was tiny, but clearly visible.

Mustering her courage, she was determined to try to explain her reasons for refusing to make love with him. She might meet with no success, but the situation between them could hardly be worse. The atmosphere in the cockpit crackled with a tension she found intolerable.

"Would you please give me a chance to explain—" she began and was able to get no further.

"It's unimportant," he cut in dismissingly, his icy gaze shooting over to her briefly before swinging away.

"To you perhaps, but not to me," she disagreed firmly, determined not to give up no matter how he provoked her. "I was really turned on down there. I wanted you to make love to me. Surely you could tell that for yourself." Deep down she still found this admission more than a little shocking. *Was it true that a woman's sexuality strengthens in her thirties and forties?* she wondered with one part of her mind as she continued. "You have to realize that I've never been to bed with any man but Paul, and it just seems *wrong* to go to bed with somebody I'm not married to. That's terribly old-fashioned, I know, but I was brought up to think that way. So were you, but society is inclined to excuse men for breaking the rules. Please—I hope you'll believe me—there was no snobbery involved in my turning you down."

This last was delivered with fervor that should have left no doubt of her sincerity, and she implored him with her eyes and expression to believe her. He hadn't looked over at her while she talked, but now he scrutinized her face at some length before turning his gaze upward again to the sails. Unexpectedly he smiled, a wry self-deprecating smile.

"Don't worry about it," he said quietly. "I overreacted. You're right about the chip on my shoulder. It's there, all right, and I've gotten so used to it, it feels comfortable. I'm probably the one to apologize. I shouldn't have made a pass at you in the first place. You can be sure it won't happen again."

His candor and the reasonableness of his attitude made her feel worse rather than better. Contradictorily she felt more regret than relief that her brain had overruled the desires of her body and stopped Burt from making love to her. After all, Paul was living with another woman, sharing her bed and satisfying his sexual needs. Why should Charlene continue to remain faithful to him? Even as she remembered the touch of Burt's hands on her body, the deep passion of his kiss, her heartbeat quickened and she wondered what it would have been like to make love with him. All her womanly instincts told her he would be a skillful lover. . . .

Cutting off this disruptive train of thought, she reminded herself that it was unlikely now that she would ever discover if her intuition about Burt's prowess as a lover was true. He had said, "You can be sure it won't happen again." Under the circumstances, it was probably for the best. She hadn't given up all hope of a reconciliation with Paul yet, and with her conventional upbringing, she might feel guilty about sleeping with a man she wasn't married to.

There was little conversation on the return sail,

but the atmosphere was no longer tense. They seemed to have attained a state of truce for the time being. Charlene felt a ridiculous sense of partnership with him when Burt asked her to take over the tiller while he lowered the sails. Watching him as he moved with lithe assurance around the deck, she appreciated the smooth, efficient play of muscles in his wiry body and remembered the touch of his flesh under her hands, the tautness of his male frame against her softer feminine contours. Guilt or no guilt at the thought of intimacy with a man other than her husband, a little shiver of pleasure rippled across her skin at the memory.

"Stay there. You're doing fine," he ordered briskly when he returned to the cockpit and she moved to turn the tiller back over to him. The matter-of-fact approval might have been lavish praise the way it warmed her insides. She concentrated upon maintaining a course right up the center of the river.

Chapter Four

There's no need to let me off here," Charlene demurred when she saw that Burt was steering the boat toward the fuel dock. "I'll help you tie up and walk back from your slip. The exercise will do me good."

"I need to top off my fuel tank anyway," Burt explained, not changing his direction.

Something about the way his eyes searched the fuel dock and the front porch of the house made her uneasy, but she brushed aside the feeling, telling herself she was being silly. There was no cause for alarm just because Cappy hadn't appeared at the sound of Burt's engine, as she and Burt both knew he would have done had he been within hearing range. He had an uncanny ability to recognize almost any boat in the marina by the sound of its engine. He was probably attending to some little job or visiting with somebody inside the marina away from the river.

In spite of these reassurances, Charlene's heart-beat quickened with apprehension as she followed Burt's instructions and took two cylindrical rubber fenders from a cockpit locker and hung them in place over the side of the boat. *Stop being such a worrywart!* she scolded herself firmly. Cappy was probably fine. Possibly he had even driven over into Madisonville— But no, there was his two-toned green pickup parked in its usual place, and the door of the store was wide open.

"Cap-py!"

The fear she couldn't quite banish in spite of all her efforts to rationalize it away made her voice crack as she called out her grandfather's name when the boat was coming alongside the fuel dock. Further down the river she could hear the echo and then another fainter one, farther away. The repetition of her own voice had a weirdly mocking quality that sent her inner terror soaring.

"CAPPY!" she yelled again, louder this time. Jumping from the boat to the fuel dock, she left Burt with the task of tying up the boat. No doubt he thought she was behaving strangely, but she didn't care. She had a powerful compulsion to locate Cappy at once and make sure he was all right. Nothing else was important.

"Charly, see if he's in the house. I'll check the office," Burt ordered brusquely before she had taken more than two steps toward the open door of the store. Abruptly she pivoted to her right and half-ran along the fuel dock to the steps leading up to the porch of the house.

"Cappy! Cappy!" she kept calling, the hysterical note in her voice increasing the nightmarish certainty that something terrible was wrong with her grandfather. Burt thought so, too. She had detected the fear underneath the terseness of his voice.

By the time she had reached the screen door opening from the living room out onto the front porch, her heart was pounding so hard she felt faint and her knees wobbled under her. Jerking open the door, she walked inside the house and stood still a second, inhaling deeply and trying to calm herself. She couldn't just fall to pieces like this. After all, she didn't know for *sure*—

"Cappy," she called hoarsely, her voice barely more than a whisper as she walked quickly across the living room to the door of the kitchen and glanced inside to see what she already knew deep inside. Cappy wasn't in there. He wasn't in his bedroom, either, or the bathroom or her own bedroom, but she looked inside each of the rooms anyway, her breathing and the tap of her sandals the only sound in the chilling quietness.

Completely heedless of her own safety, Charlene left the house, the screen door slamming behind her, and ran the distance along the porch to the steps, leaped down them to the fuel dock and rushed to the open door of the store. Something kept her from calling out Cappy's name now, something aside from the sheer impossibility of producing sound through a throat knotted and paralyzed by overwhelming fear.

Burt met her at the door of the office, his body blocking her entry. She pushed against him and struggled to get past him, to no avail, but she did manage to ascertain that Cappy was inside the office. He lay on his back on the floor, his face gray and utterly lifeless. Cappy was—

"Charly! You've got to get hold of yourself!"

Burt's low, urgent voice penetrated her consciousness and made her aware for the first time that the strange whimpering sounds she heard were coming from *her.* Collapsing against him, all the fight ebbing from her, she burrowed her face into his chest and searched within herself for strength and courage to ask the question whose answer she had seen for herself.

"Is he . . . is he . . . ?" she asked in a voice so muffled that he might not be able to distinguish the words.

"No, Charly, he *isn't*—" Burt said firmly, taking her by the shoulders and forcing her back from him a few inches so that he could speak the words into her face, as if to give them greater force. Later when Charlene would go back over the scene in her mind, she would remember that Burt hadn't been able to said the dreaded word, with all its finality, any more than she could.

"He's had another stroke, but he's alive," Burt continued, still speaking slowly and with emphasis. "I've called for an ambulance. It should be here in a few minutes. In the meantime, you've got to pull yourself together. I want you to change clothes and ride to the hospital in the ambulance with Cappy. I'll have to take care of my boat, but I'll come to the hospital as fast as I can. Now *go*. There's no time to waste. We have to think about what's best for Cappy." He turned her around and gave her a little push toward the door.

Charlene obeyed numbly, without any further questions or any protests. Even in her present state of mind, mentally and emotionally devastated as she was, she spoke a little prayer of thanks that Burt was there to take charge. What if he hadn't decided to stop at the fuel dock and *she* had been the one to discover Cappy, the one who would have had to put aside personal feelings and act quickly for Cappy's welfare? She preferred not to think of that possibility now. Burt was right when he said they had to concentrate on what was best for Cappy. She would summon all her strength for whatever lay ahead.

This resolution took her through the nightmare of the next hour. Somehow she changed her clothes and made herself presentable, and then watched as Cappy was transferred with gentle, efficient skill from the floor of his office to the ambulance. She rode the short distance to the parish hospital with the sound of the siren filling her head, thankful the hospital was less than ten miles from the marina. In the emergency room's waiting room, she sat tensely for what seemed like endless hours, wishing for some encouraging report on Cappy's condition.

"Oh, thank God you're here," she murmured when Burt came into the waiting room.

"Any word yet?" he asked quietly.

Shaking her head in a negative answer, Charlene tried to muster a smile to reassure him. She could see the worry in his eyes, the anxiety underlying his tense composure.

"He's going to be all right, Burt," she murmured. "He's *got* to be all right."

As Burt sat down in the chair next to hers, Charlene was suffused with an entirely illogical hope. With both Burt and herself together in the waiting room, his love for Cappy joining forces with her own, Cappy *would* recover. She just *knew* he would.

As if to lend support to her unscientific intuition, the emergency room doctor appeared almost immediately, the expression on his countenance indicating that the news he bore was positive. Cappy was being transferred to intensive care; his vital signs were encouraging. Charlene and Burt were told to wait for further word in another waiting room in a different section of the hospital.

At first the relief was so overwhelming that Charlene was buoyed along on a wave of optimism that Cappy was going to be all right. But then as an hour passed and then another, and the miraculous change in Cappy's condition didn't occur, her nerves began to fray under the strain of waiting. No longer able to sit and flip through the pages of magazines, she paced the floor of the waiting room, stopping now and then to stare at nondescript prints on the wall without even seeing them.

"Where is this partner of Cappy's now?" she

demanded without any preamble, coming back and dropping wearily on the sofa next to Burt.

He looked startled and then puzzled.

"What could *he* do unless he's a doctor?" he asked with restrained impatience.

If Charlene's emotions hadn't been so churned up by the events of the past hours, she would have recognized the question and its tone to be perfectly reasonable, but she felt anything but reasonable at the moment. Something inside her chest was raw and bruised, and she needed somebody to blame.

"This is partly *his* fault, don't you think?" she said belligerently. "He should be helping Cappy run the marina, not just putting up the money and leaving Cappy with all the work and all the headaches." Jumping up from the sofa, she paced a few steps toward the opposite wall and then whirled around, her arms folded tightly across her waist and her mouth set. "I'm going to *insist* that Cappy tell me who this person is. I'm going to get in touch with him and *tell* him just what a despicable human being he is—" Her voice broke and she pressed a fist against her lips to try to control their trembling. She could feel herself dangerously on the verge of tears.

Burt got up swiftly from the couch and came over to her with a few long strides. She didn't resist when he clasped her shoulders with hands that were strong and steady and drew her gently against his chest. As his arms closed around her, she relaxed against him, needing his strength at a time when her own supply was severely depleted.

"Charly, you know you're not making any sense,"

he chided gravely. "It's nobody else's fault this has happened to Cappy. He's an independent old cuss, and we both know it. It's one of the things we love about him. If anybody's to blame, it's Cappy himself. He didn't follow his doctor's advice after the first attack. But it's *his* life, and he has the right to live it the way *he* chooses."

Charlene knew he was right. If anybody were to blame other than Cappy himself, it was *her,* not the mysterious partner, whoever he was. She should have contacted Cappy's doctor herself immediately upon her arrival and found out what restriction he had placed upon Cappy's activities.

"Mrs. Reed."

Dr. Hastings' voice cut through her self-recriminations. Pulling abruptly away from Burt's supportive embrace, she turned and walked toward the door of the waiting room, where her grandfather's physician stood.

"How is he, doctor?" she asked anxiously, aware that Burt had followed behind her and was waiting for the news, too.

Dr. Hastings' smile was reassurance in itself. He explained in his deep, rumbling voice that Cappy was well enough now to be taken from intensive care to a private room.

"He's under sedation and won't be allowed any visitors tonight, but by tomorrow morning—if I know that tough old customer—he'll be giving us all a hard time of it. Why don't you go on home now and get a good night's rest. You can see him in the morning. I'll be able to tell you more about his condition by then. It may take all of us to hog-tie him, but this time he's going to stay right here until he's ready to go home."

"Thank you, doctor," Charlene breathed. The fervency in her voice expressed the gratitude that flooded her whole being at the optimism the doctor conveyed. Cappy was going to be all right!

The euphoric swell of her relief made her as docile and unquestioning as a child who has just lived through a nightmarish experience and is glad to be back under the protection of an adult. She let Burt lead her from the hospital out to the parking lot, where he held open the door of his car while she climbed in on the passenger's side. The car was the same army green Volkswagen jeep she had noticed in front of his boat slip that first day.

"Would you like to get something to eat before we go back to the marina?" Burt asked when he had come around and gotten in under the wheel. "I don't know about you, but I'm hollow."

Charlene's first instinct was to refuse. It was close to eight o'clock and she, too, felt empty, but the thought of food was vaguely revolting. Later on tonight she could fix herself a sandwich or a snack—

"I don't *feel* hungry, but I should eat something, I suppose," she said quickly, her mind shifting away from its train of thought as she realized for the first time she would have to face that silent, empty little house tonight, with just the company of her own thoughts and memories and the specters of the last few hours. At least she could put off her return for another hour or two.

"Feel like eating anything in particular?" Burt inquired, twisting the key and making the engine leap noisily into life.

"Anything will be fine," Charlene said indifferently. "Hamburger, pizza, chicken. Or how about a steak?" she added, thinking that it would take longer if they went to a regular restaurant rather than to a fast-food place. "My treat."

The impulsive offer was no sooner out than she wished she could retract it. She hadn't meant to suggest that she was better able to pay for their meals than Burt was, but that's the way it had sounded. His gaze swung sharply over to her, but he didn't answer as he shifted the car into gear and drove out of the parking lot and onto the street running along the front of the hospital. He was headed into Covington rather than back toward Madisonville.

Charlene sneaked a regretful glance toward his profile, noting the aloofness and the self-assurance in his bearing. He had been a boulder, propping her up through the strain of the last four or five hours. The last thing she would want to do was hurt his feelings!

"Burt, I can't tell you how grateful I am," she said sincerely. "I just don't know what I would have *done* if you hadn't been there this afternoon—" Her voice choked as she remembered the terror of those minutes when she had searched for Cappy, certain that the very worst had happened.

"Hey, try to put all that out of your mind now," Burt ordered firmly, reaching over and giving her hand a hard squeeze. "Cappy's doing fine. Just think about that."

Charlene would have made another attempt to express her gratitude, but they had already arrived at their destination, a low, ranch-style structure with a neon sign out front blinking out the restaurant's name, RICHARD'S.

"I remember this place, but it used to be Brown's. Right? Didn't it just serve huge, homestyle meals, whatever they happened to cook that day?"

The questions were mainly rhetorical, and without waiting for an answer, Charlene opened her own door and got out of the car. She was determined not to make another *faux pas* that would erect old barriers between them.

"It hasn't been Brown's for years," Burt informed her as they walked to the front door. "Now it's kind of a compromise between fast-food and a regular restaurant. You can order take-out at the inside window or you can sit down at a table and have a waitress serve you. The food is good either way, particularly the seafood."

Inside the restaurant, he led her to a table against the right-hand wall. Charlene relaxed, relieved that his voice had held no nuance to indicate that he was offended at her earlier offer to buy his dinner. She certainly would not bring the subject up again if he didn't.

The bright lighting cheered rather than irritated her, and she glanced around at the plain, unpretentious decor before consulting the menu. The dull emptiness in her stomach was sharpening into hunger pangs, and she had a hard time deciding what to order, settling finally upon a cup of seafood gumbo and a shrimp po-boy.

"Hmmmmm. You're right—the food *is* good here," she approved after tasting the thick, savory gumbo served over rice. When her shrimp po-boy arrived, the French bread was crusty and fresh and the shrimp large and cooked perfectly, still chewy and succulent.

Aside from appreciative comments about the food, they talked little during the meal. Burt ate his fried oyster dinner with undisguised relish and downed several beers. He finished before she did and watched her as she lifted the French bread from the second half of her po-boy sandwich and picked off the shrimp. Finishing the last one, she rolled her eyes upward in exaggerated bliss.

"It feels so sinful," she said confidentially, "eating rice and French bread and fried shrimp all in one meal. Tomorrow it'll be back to salad and something broiled."

Heaving a big sigh of satisfaction, she sat back in her chair, smiling at him with the faintest trace of wistfulness. Without overdoing things, she wanted him to know she appreciated his choice of restaurants.

Involuntarily she sucked in her breath as she noted the shift of his gaze down to the front of her blouse, where the small mounds of her breasts were lifted against the soft fabric. The moment hovered delicately on the brink of sexual awareness. All he had to do was murmur some comment about the results of her scrupulous attention to diet and exercise or simply lift his eyes to meet hers and force the mutual awareness that he was a man and she a woman. Instead, he reached inside his hip pocket and took out his wallet. Extracting a bill, he laid it on the check the waitress had left lying on the table.

"Ready?" he asked without looking directly at her, at the same time pushing back his chair and standing up.

Charlene stifled a flare of irritation she didn't entirely understand. The furthest thing from her mind was trying to seduce Burt, for heaven's sake! But there was no reason a man and a woman couldn't find each other attractive and enjoy the spice of sexuality in their relationship without feeling they had to go to bed together. Burt seemed to begrudge her even the tacit compliment of admitting he was aware of her female attractions.

She mulled over these mildly resentful reflections during most of the drive home, but when he turned off the highway onto the shell-covered road to the marina, suddenly the reality of the present struck with a chilling impact. Cappy was lying in the hospital tonight, sedated. He wouldn't sit in front of the television set tonight arguing with the newscasters or insulting the weatherman. Tomorrow morning he wouldn't awaken her with the clanking of the components of the coffee pot as he made his potent brew. His vital, colorful presence would fill the house and haunt her with his absence.

"Would you come in for a while? I could make some coffee—or maybe you'd rather a drink. I'm sure Cappy must have some whiskey," she invited urgently when Burt pulled up in front of Cappy's house and waited for her to get out, the engine still running.

Burt looked across at her in the darkness, refusal etched in the sternness of his shadowy features. Whatever conclusions he might draw about her motives, Charlene was suddenly desperate to keep him from driving away and leaving her to go alone into Cappy's house. She wasn't physically afraid. The house would be safer than her house in Atlanta was from the danger of burglars or rapists, but the thought of facing its emptiness was turning the food in her stomach into a dense, heavy mass. She wished now she hadn't eaten that large meal.

"Please," she begged simply. "Just for a little while."

He reached for the key with an abrupt movement and turned it, killing the engine. Charlene thrust open her door and got out, her knees shaky with relief.

Inside the house she wasted no time in switching on lights and turning on the television. Burt watched her as she flitted around with hurried movements.

"Sit down," she urged, trying to produce a cheerful smile and then finding to her utter dismay that her lips were not obeying the dictate of her brain. Instead of curving, they quivered in little convulsions, and tears ached in her throat. Her whole body had begun to tremble alarmingly so that she knew she had better sit down somewhere quickly or run the risk of finding herself in a heap on the floor.

"I'm sor—" she began, but the apology was engulfed by the sobs that suddenly shook her. There seemed to be no stopping the inexplicable storm of emotion sweeping her. She didn't know *why* she was crying. Cappy was going to be all right.

When Burt came over and put his arms around her and tried to soothe her, she cried even harder.

"I'm sorry," she said after a while when the sobs seemed to lessen of their own volition and she was able to assert some control over her emotions. "That took me completely by surprise, too." Her tone, like the face she lifted from his shoulder, held rueful apology.

"It's just a reaction to the last few hours," Burt asserted calmly, keeping one arm around her shoulders as he drew her over to the sofa. "Nature's way of restoring equilibrium."

Nothing in his tone indicated that he thought her weak for breaking down the way she had, but Charlene was embarrassed nonetheless. He had seen her at her most vulnerable.

"I've always prided myself on not being a weepy, hysterical type," she said with an attempt at humor, her voice still husky from the recent tears. "You were just as worried about Cappy this afternoon as I was, and you didn't get *my* shoulder all wet." This last was literally true. Her tears had soaked through the blue chambray of his shirt to form a dark patch.

The expression in his blue eyes was bleakly honest as they met and held hers. His mouth was twisted with irony as he spoke.

"Why do you think I didn't want to come in this

house tonight? I was going to let you face this alone. That's not exactly manly courage, is it?"

Charlene felt as though the revelation about himself drew her closer to him than she had ever been before. It took courage for him to admit openly he wasn't as invincible as he appeared, after all. She admired him now more than she had before she knew the truth.

"Thank you for telling me," she said softly, and then feeling that comic relief would be the best thing for both of them at that moment, added laughingly, "If you hadn't agreed to come in for something to drink tonight, I wouldn't have gotten out of your car! You'd have ended up with an overnight guest aboard your boat!"

The furthest thing from her mind was to be provocative, but the moment the words were out his eyes took on an electric intensity, as though a light had been ignited inside them. His gaze skimmed over her slender form clad in dusky rose slacks and long-sleeved print blouse and came back to her face, holding her spellbound within a current of awareness. Her eyes were red from weeping and her cheeks stained with tears, but under his inspection she had never felt more feminine and alluring. Then abruptly he turned his head away and broke the pulsing contact.

"How about that drink you offered?" he asked abruptly, fixing his eyes on the television screen.

It took her a second or two to make the necessary adjustment. During that time she felt the same surge of irritation she had experienced earlier that evening in the restaurant. Why was Burt so unwilling for her to see that he was attracted to her?

"Sure," she said finally, getting up and going over to the television set to turn up the volume. "What would you like? Whiskey or coffee? There's beer in the refrigerator, too, of course."

"I'll take a beer then," he said without taking his gaze off the screen, as though fascinated with the images flickering across it. Charlene automatically looked at it herself and saw that some sort of chase scene was in progress, a whole fleet of police cars pursuing a red van.

By the time she returned with his beer and a whiskey and water on the rocks for herself, the ten o'clock news was on. The channel was the same one Cappy watched every night. Charlene was grateful for the mere fact of Burt's presence even if he did seem entirely unaware of her as she sat next to him on the sofa and sipped her drink, trying hard to make her mind concentrate on the news. She kept seeing Cappy the way he had looked that afternoon, so gray and lifeless.

When Burt had finished the beer, she promptly offered him another, but he refused. A hard tension gripped her stomach as she watched the station's meteorologist stand in front of a luridly colored map of the United States and point to various curving lines and symbols. Not a word of his forecast penetrated her consciousness. She was trying to cope with the realization that the news program was almost over now and Burt would be leaving. She would be alone in the house with the silence . . . with her memories and thoughts . . .

"Burt, please don't leave me by myself here tonight," she blurted out, without any preamble.

His gaze swung sharply to her face, and he stared at her for a long moment.

"You want me to *stay* here with you?" he asked carefully.

"Would you? Just for one night?" she pleaded.

He got up abruptly and went over to snap off the television set. His expression told her nothing as he came back to take his same place next to her on the sofa.

"Charly," he began in a patient voice, "Cappy's going to be in the hospital quite a while. You do realize that, don't you? If you're afraid to stay here in the house, maybe you should go to a motel. But I think you're safe—"

"I know all that!" she interrupted. "I'm not scared in the way you think." She hesitated, overcoming the reluctance to speak her real fears out loud. "It's hard to explain," she said slowly, lifting her eyes to meet his and then dropping them again to her hands, tightly interlaced in her lap. "All my life I seemed to have needed people around me . . . lots of people. It's so easy for me to meet people wherever I go, to make friends. Every time Paul and I would move to a new place, I didn't waste one second getting to know my neighbors. But Cappy is the only person in the whole world who *really* cares about me. He's the only one I'm terribly *important to*—"

She swallowed hard, trying to deal with an obstruction in her throat that grew larger by the second. "When I called out his name this afternoon and he didn't answer . . . When I saw him lying on the floor like that in the office—" Charlene buried her face in her hands, finding it impossible to continue. She couldn't bear to say aloud what she had thought during those terrifying moments.

"Charly, he's going to be all right," Burt assured her brusquely, the roughness of his tone betraying his own emotion.

When he moved to put his arms around her, Charlene turned toward him instinctively, slipping her arms around his waist and hugging him close to her with all her strength. She desperately needed his human warmth and comfort, needed them too much to worry about pride. For a long moment they stayed just as they were, not speaking and holding each other so tightly Charlene imagined she could feel the shape of his bones under the vital, warm flesh. His heart beat steadily into her own chest.

"I suppose it's hard for you to understand someone like me," she reflected aloud. "You don't need people at all, do you? You like being alone."

He didn't answer at once. The quality of the silence told her he was examining her words, which had been a simple statement of fact with no resentment or accusation to make him defensive.

"I don't know that anyone doesn't need people *at all,*" he said finally, "or that I necessarily *like* being alone." He was faltering for the right words, just as she had a moment ago when she tried to define for him the nature of her fears. "It's just that for certain people, being alone is the safest course. One doesn't get . . . involved."

The moment was too delicate for comment or for further questions. She mulled over what he had just told her, knowing he probably had never told another human being what was deeply buried inside him, causing him to live the life of a loner. His philosophy was strikingly alien to her own. He considered the company of other people "dangerous" while to her solitude presented the ultimate kind of test of one's strengths and resources. Wasn't it strange that what she perceived as a strength in Burt, his absolute self-sufficiency, he construed as a kind of cowardice. She admired his ability to be alone with himself, and here he was suggesting that he felt too vulnerable to allow himself to become involved with people.

The irony of the present situation struck her forcibly. Her needs and Burt's were in direct conflict tonight. By his own admission, he hadn't wanted to come in with her tonight because the ghost of Cappy's presence would be here to haunt him. He had wanted to go to the privacy—hence, the safety— of his boat, but she hadn't let him do that, out of her own selfish needs. Probably he needed to be alone tonight to recover from the trauma of today's events as much as she needed *not* to be alone.

It was as though the glimpse into Burt's private soul served as an infusion of much-needed courage. Charlene decided that in just a few moments—as soon as she could force herself to draw away from the pure comfort of his closeness—she would send him on his way. But not just yet.

"Thank you for everything," she murmured, moving the palm of one hand along his back, her intent being to convey the gratitude and deep human sympathy she felt toward him at this moment. The muscles were hard and smooth, tightening involuntarily under the gentle stroking movement of her hand. For a second or two, his whole body tensed as though it wanted to reject her touch, but then his own hand was sliding along her back, creating a hot friction between the tough skin of his palm and the thin silken material of her blouse. His hand would make fractional pauses, allowing his strong fingers to knead the responsive firmness of her flesh. His touch felt wonderful to her, and she sighed aloud her intense pleasure.

Now both her hands ensued upon a thorough exploration of his back and shoulders, delighting in the smooth hardness of the contours. The new intimacy she felt toward Burt, freeing her to touch his body as she was doing, was mental as well as physical. He was someone she had known for years and yet hadn't known at all before now. A delicate sense of discovery trembled inside her, a subdued exhilaration she had never known before and thus couldn't readily identify. It was extremely fragile, though, and she wanted to protect it from Burt's sudden spurt of anger as he muttered a savage curse and thrust her away from him, the once gentle hands cruel as they bit into the flesh of her shoulders.

"What's the matter?" she protested helplessly, staring into his face, whose features were distorted with anger.

"You just can't help yourself, can you?" he bit out between clenched teeth. "You get some kind of perverted pleasure out of turning me on and then off again." The blue eyes glared into her dazed, blinking brown ones.

When the reason for his fury finally dawned upon her, the first disappointment was overwhelming. He saw no difference between their relationship now and what it had been earlier in the afternoon when she had refused to make love with him on the boat out on the lake. Couldn't he sense that everything had changed? What she felt for him tonight was more than sex, and it hurt to know he simply thought her a callous little tease. She would prove to him he was wrong.

His eyes narrowed suspiciously as she lifted her hands slowly to his face and framed the rigid angles of his jawline. He seemed tense and ready to jerk his head away from her soft touch, but he remained absolutely still, watching her as she brought her lips to his and kissed him, tentatively at first, savoring the shape and feel of his lips with the same sense of discovery she'd felt while exploring his back with her hands. His mouth was passive under hers for long seconds, but when her fingertips slid down to lightly caress the rigid cords of his neck, the restraint holding him snapped.

The hands still gripping her shoulders tightened convulsively for a painful moment and then slid down her back, pulling her to him. As his arms tightened around her, his mouth moved with a desperate hunger against hers, the low sounds reverberating in his throat like trapped protests against a passion he couldn't control. His tongue thrust between her soft, parted lips and found hers, engaging it in an intimacy so bold and sweet that she moaned, her hands slipping up around his neck and pulling his head toward her with a pressure that was hardly necessary since his lips were already bruising hers with their hard urgency.

It was altogether natural for Burt to press her back upon the cushions of the sofa. Certainly she wouldn't have thought of resisting, not with the weight of his frame lowered on top of hers, the thrust of his hips and aggressive maleness against her pelvic cradle awakening to throbbing life her own sexual need, a need she had kept suppressed for more than just the weeks of her separation from Paul. She moaned and moved under Burt, accepting the weight of his body and welcoming the stimulation of what it promised.

Dragging his mouth aside from hers, he muttered her name, his breathing labored. Charlene smiled a bemused smile, letting her eyes meet him unfalteringly to allow him to see whatever there was in their depths. She was pretending nothing, concealing nothing. For a breathtaking moment, the blue eyes staring down at her were lit by a brilliant light, taking her breath away with the strange intensity, but then he lowered his gaze to her breasts and fumbled with the buttons of her blouse, freeing them finally and thrusting aside the material to bring her breasts, in their lacy captivity, into full view.

Bending his head, he kissed the valley between them. Then he raised himself up long enough to deal with the front clasp of her bra. As he slowly peeled the lacy covering away, Charlene felt the air on her exposed flesh. The sensation was erotic in itself. That and the anticipation of his descending head made her nipples tingle and harden even before his mouth closed, warm and moist, around the tip of one breast. His tongue was rough and sent little piercing shocks of pleasure through her entire body. The pleasant ache in her pelvis sharpened into something more insistent, and she lifted her hips against the grinding weight of his.

Murmuring his name, she ran her palms along the planes of his back down to the waistband of his slacks, where she pulled his shirt free and reached up under it to feel his bare flesh. He paused for a second in his attentions to her breasts, quivering as she raked her fingernails lightly across his skin.

When he raised himself up and sat on the edge of the sofa, looking down at her with an expression that was dazed with his aroused passion, she knew he must see something similar on her own features. Perhaps he was expecting some kind of refusal as he reached for the waistband of her slacks, but none was forthcoming. Instead she helped him, lifting her hips as he tugged the slacks down past them and then free of her legs.

While he stood and began to strip off his clothes, slowly, without taking his eyes off her, she shed her blouse and bra and the lacy wisp of her bikini panties. Naked, she lay there and looked up at him, meeting his eyes and seeing there, along with the blue flame of his passion, his recognition that she hadn't been playing with him, that she wouldn't draw back at the last moment as he had evidently expected.

As he bent over her, bracing his weight on hands placed on either side of her, she closed her eyes with the anticipation and then gasped aloud at the sheer ecstasy of his deep, surging entry. Lifting her legs, she locked them around his waist, opening her body to him and lifting her hips to absorb his thrusts, to carry them deeper within her, the pleasure so piercing she could hardly bear it. With her hands she caressed his back and shoulders, murmuring aloud the mounting sense of joy as he lifted her from one level of sensual pleasure to another, higher and higher to the pinnacle and its excruciating release.

Afterwards they both seemed too dazed to be capable of speech, each of them absorbed in private reflections. Charlene was amazed at her total lack of inhibition and was a little embarrassed. *Maybe that old myth about increased sexuality in maturing women was true after all,* she mused, and sneaked a glance over at Burt, who sat sprawled on the sofa beside her, one arm loosely around her shoulders. His head was tilted back and his eyes closed. A feeling of tenderness swept Charlene as she saw the weariness in his profile.

Acting on impulse, she leaned over and dropped a quick little kiss on his cheek. His eyes flew open, revealing an expression so disconcertingly strange that she drew back a fraction, concluding that he had been asleep and she had startled him.

"Why don't you go on to your boat now," she suggested. "You look like you could use some sleep."

He sat up straight, withdrawing his arm from around her. She immediately regretted the loss of his warmth and weight, heavy though it had been.

"I'll sleep right here," he said decisively. "This sofa is as comfortable as my bunk."

She gave his intention some consideration, struggling with a selfish instinct to allow him to stay with her in the house tonight. It was true she would like to have him here with her, but she didn't want him to think there were strings attached to her having made love with him.

"That won't be necessary," she said finally. "You said yourself you thought I'd be perfectly safe here."

He hesitated, apparently torn between what he actually preferred to do and what he thought would be best for her.

"If you don't mind, I'd feel better sleeping right here tonight," he said resolutely, having made his decision.

Her resistance had been a token one from the beginning. She had only been trying to be unselfish by urging Burt to return to his boat for the night.

"Of course, I don't mind," she scoffed. "But I see no reason you should sleep on the sofa—" She broke off, taken aback by the sharpness of his gaze and the frown cutting little ridges between his eyebrows.

"You don't think I could sleep in Cappy's bed—not after—" He couldn't complete the harsh objection.

"I wasn't suggesting you sleep in Cappy's bedroom," she spoke up quickly, wanting to correct his error. "You can sleep with me in my bed." She shrugged, letting her expression convey what should be obvious to both of them: they might as well share a bed since they had already shared the most intimate act a man and woman can perform together.

The prospect of sleeping with her in her bed evidently presented some problems to Burt. She watched the struggle on his face with a mixture of emotions, among them bafflement and hurt until she reminded herself of what he had revealed earlier when they both were baring their souls. Burt's aloofness went below the surface. While she couldn't understand what there was about sleeping in a bed with her that threatened his solitary way of life, she owed him too much gratitude to press him into doing something he chose not to do. Arriving at this resolution, she stood up and announced pleasantly, "You can suit yourself, of course. If sleeping on the sofa is more what you're used to, then be my guest. I'll get some sheets and a pillow."

The spare linen was kept in the bathroom closet along with the towels and washcloths. When she returned to the living room with the sheets, Burt wasn't there. The sound of running water out in the kitchen told her he had evidently gone for a glass of water. She wondered ruefully if he had indeed been thirsty or if he were trying to avoid her.

When she had spread the sheets on the sofa and made a trip to her bedroom for a pillow and a blanket, Burt still hadn't returned, his absence seeming to prove her hypothesis that he was avoiding her. She could either out-wait him or she could go on to bed. She decided on the latter.

When she came out of the bathroom a few minutes later, having brushed her teeth and cleaned her face, a glance toward the living room verified that it was dark. Burt had turned out the lights and was lying in there on his makeshift bed he preferred to sleep in alone.

"Good night, Burt," she called softly toward the darkness, but there was no answer.

With a little sigh of acceptance, she went on into her bedroom and slipped on a nightgown before getting into bed. Suddenly she was terribly exhausted and wanted nothing but to sink into the dark oblivion of sleep. Burt's silent presence out there was deeply reassuring. She was glad he had insisted upon staying.

Chapter Five

Charlene pushed the manila folder back down into its place and closed the filing cabinet drawer. A self-derogatory little smile lifted the corners of her mouth as she realized she had been eavesdropping, straining her ears to hear every word of the conversation between Burt and the Dixie beer delivery man outside in the store. The exchange was a perfectly normal one, beginning with the delivery man's inquiries about Cappy's health and progressing from there to current events with emphasis on the problems of the national economy. She could tell Burt was wishing the garrulous fellow would be on his way, but chatting with deliverymen was part of the job of running a small store like this one.

Even though her work was finished for the day,

she put off going outside into the store, knowing her appearance would only delay the man's departure. Instead she tidied up the surface of the old desk, arranging the few papers into orderly stacks, letting her mind drift over the past week and a half. What would she have done without Burt during that time, with Cappy in the hospital and herself in charge of the marina and the store? Until now she just hadn't appreciated the multiplicity of details involved in the day-to-day running of a fuel dock and marina, not to mention the store. Cappy had always made the whole operation look so effortless.

She would have gotten by without Burt if he hadn't just happened to be living in the marina at this time, but she was frankly grateful she hadn't found it necessary to muddle through on her own. And with the Mardi Gras boat parade coming up this weekend, she was doubly glad for his help. It was one of the busiest times of the entire year on the river, rivaling the Fourth of July and Labor Day.

On Monday Cappy would be discharged from the hospital and coming home. She would be depending heavily on Burt's support to make that stubborn old customer follow the doctor's orders and take it easy for several more weeks until he had his strength back. It had been anything but easy to keep him in the hospital this long. The whole hospital staff would probably heave a collective sigh of relief when he was gone!

The Dixie beer man was finally leaving now. Charlene glanced down at her watch and saw that it was time to lock up for the day. Walking from the office out into the store, she stopped in the middle of the room and watched for a few seconds as Burt counted the money in the cash register. Taking care of the money was one of the tasks he had simply assumed without being asked. If there happened to be more than he deemed safe to be kept on the premises, locked in the old, black iron wall safe in Cappy's office, he would make a night deposit at the Madisonville bank. He would make one tonight, she presumed, since they had had a fairly busy day.

Quite a few boatowners had already arrived in the marina, eager to get an early start on preparations and partying. The fuel dock had done a good business and so had the store, with sales of ice and beer and snack foods running high. Tomorrow would be a madhouse and Sunday even worse. Sunday, the marina would be jammed with cars and people, and you wouldn't be able to see the river for the boats churning up the water.

"We'll need a good supply of change for tomorrow," she suggested, sauntering over to the cash register, fingertips thrust into the back pockets of her jeans.

He nodded without looking up, slipping a rubber band around a stack of bills.

"Bank's open until six tonight. Thought I'd pick up some extra rolls of change when I make this deposit. By nine o'clock tomorrow morning, it'll be hell getting across that drawbridge into town."

Charlene noted the irritation in his voice and didn't find it surprising. Burt wasn't looking forward to the hectic weekend at all. The urge was strong to tell him to relax and enjoy the mayhem, as she intended to do, but then she caught herself. She had to keep reminding herself that she and Burt were two entirely different personality types. She loved being around people, all kinds of people, whether she had anything in common with them or not. Burt was a loner. He'd much prefer to be by himself than in the company of people he didn't particularly like, and he made no bones about declaring his opinion of the powerboat owners in the marina, most of whom did tend to be a little on the boisterous side, especially when they were drinking. He considered them a "bunch of boring fools."

Watching the smooth, efficient movement of his hands as he dealt with the contents of the cash register, she knew after a week and a half of working closely with him why there was no jerky, wasted motion. Burt's brain always functioned well in advance of his body. His every action was decisive.

She had been amazed the first couple of days, having assumed that the major yoke of responsibility would rest on her shoulders since she was Cappy's flesh and blood. A deliveryman would arrive and while she was running to the file cabinet to check invoices, undecided as to what she should order, Burt would walk in and tell the man they would take two cases of potato chips and one of corn chips and to be sure and remove all the old packages. He also took full responsibility for overseeing the final stages of the renovation work in the marina, which was finished now.

By the end of the second day they were running the marina together, and she had concluded that it was a crime for someone of his intelligence and apparently native business acumen to be drifting around unemployed and doing nothing constructive. He was even much quicker than she was in figuring out the bookkeeping system, and she couldn't imagine that he had ever done office work.

"Guess I'd better get up to the hospital and do what I can to soothe the caged lion," she announced lightly, as he picked up the deposit bag and began to transfer the money into it.

"Tell him I'll see him tomorrow night," Burt said briefly, zipping up the bag.

Charlene's shoulders drooped a little, but she bit back the words that would convey her disappointment. She had hoped Burt would be coming to the hospital later tonight. After visiting hours, the two of them might have gone somewhere for supper. But obviously he had other plans, and she dared not question him. That would go against their unspoken code.

"I'll tell him," she said as cheerfully as she could and started for the door on the river side. Pausing when she had reached it, she turned and looked back. "See you in the morning bright and early?" It was her last shot at giving him an opportunity to suggest seeing her *before* tomorrow morning, but he didn't even look around at her.

"Sure thing. I'll lock up."

There was nothing for her to do but make her exit.

As she walked along the fuel dock and climbed the steps to the front porch of the house, she told herself again she should be glad Burt hadn't turned out to be a problem. The next day after Cappy's stroke, she had sat with her grandfather most of the day and divided her thoughts between worrying about him and regretting her actions of the previous night. What if Burt got the wrong idea and thought she was open to some kind of serious relationship between them? She'd have to refuse him again and run the risk of inflicting even more injury. Even if her divorce went through, Charlene couldn't see herself adapting to Burt's life-style or accepting his sense of values.

By that evening she had decided that her best course was to get things straight between herself and Burt at once. She had enjoyed their lovemaking and didn't feel guilty about it under the circumstances, but it would be better for the same thing not to recur. Walking out of the hospital with him after visiting hours were over, she had braced herself to make some excuse if he suggested the two of them go somewhere and eat.

His Volkswagen jeep was parked several places down from her sleek little silver Audi sedan, but the parking spaces between the two vehicles were empty now. Charlene thought the contrast between the two cars was overwhelmingly significant, indicating two different points of view, two different life-styles. Burt's automobile was starkly plain and functional while hers suggested luxury and comfort. Her resolve not to become any further involved with Burt hardened.

"I'm beat," she said tiredly, unlocking the door on the driver's side of her car. "It's a bath and bed for me tonight."

"Sitting in a hospital all day is no fun," he said sympathetically. "But Cappy seems to be coming along fine."

Charlene couldn't detect the least hint of anything in his voice to suggest disappointment or resentment that she had indicated no desire to spend the remainder of the evening with him. It was only nine o'clock and early by her standards.

"The doctor says he's doing great," she agreed. "In fact, he won't need somebody with him every minute tomorrow. He insisted I stay at the marina and help you run things there. Thanks so much for looking after things today, Burt."

"I'm glad to do anything to help Cappy out," he said with a shrug and started walking toward his car. Then suddenly he stopped. "I almost forgot," he called over his shoulder. "I have something for you."

Charlene's heart dropped with a thud. Surely Burt hadn't gone out and bought her a present! And she had been congratulating herself on how well she had handled matters just now, discouraging any hopes he might have had concerning her without hurting his feelings.

He got something from the front seat of his car and brought it to her. She stared at the object in his hand for several seconds before she took it. A boat horn! The kind attached to a can of compressed gas. When you squeezed the rubber bulb, the thing would emit a deafening blast.

"If anybody tries to break in the house, just sound this thing off in an SOS," he explained. "It won't take me long to get there."

"Why, that's an ingenious idea!" she exclaimed. "Just the noise would probably scare a burglar to death."

She wasn't just being polite. It *was* a clever idea, and she appreciated Burt's thoughtfulness. But at the same time, it definitely rankled that while she had been searching her brain all day for some way to let him down easy, he had been devising a way to make her feel safe without having to stay in the same house with her!

A half hour later she sat in front of the television, munching a sandwich and sipping a diet soft drink, wondering what would have happened differently if she *hadn't* declared she was tired and made it plain she desired no company that evening. Probably nothing, she had to admit. Her instincts told her Burt hadn't had any intention of asking her out to eat or of trying to initiate a replay of last evening's lovemaking. What she didn't understand about herself was why she wasn't heaving a sigh of relief instead of feeling irked.

The next day she had visited Cappy briefly in the morning, found him impossibly irascible about being "cooped up in a damned hospital," and gladly escaped back to the marina at his bidding. That afternoon when she and Burt were closing up the store, she had thought ahead to her evening with a pang of loneliness. She would spend a couple of hours with Cappy at the hospital and then come home to watch television or read.

"I'll cook dinner for you tonight after visiting hours are over at the hospital," she offered almost diffidently, more than halfway expecting him to refuse.

"Sounds like a winner," he replied, accepting the invitation as casually as she had extended it.

Since then she had come to realize how needless were those original fears that Burt would become emotionally involved with her or make demands she wouldn't be willing to satisfy. He made no demands of any kind, no presumptions—but he expected the same consideration from her. If they both felt like sharing a meal or an evening, they did. If either one of them was not so inclined, a refusal was not to be accompanied by an explanation. That one did not *want* to do something was explanation enough. Charlene had the irksome suspicion that their sexual intimacy was like everything else about their relationship—Burt had no intention of allowing it to become *necessary* for him.

It was baffling for her to comprehend that one could be so complete in oneself as he was. Burt needed no one. And yet, his self-sufficiency in no way kept him from being kind and considerate to other people as long as they didn't threaten his privacy. The same rule applied to her, too, as she quickly learned. That was why she didn't press Burt tonight for an explanation of his plans or try to force her company upon him, even though she didn't look forward to the thought of being alone.

As she entered the house and headed for the bathroom, intending to shower and change before going to the hospital, the telephone rang. It was Paul. After he had inquired about Cappy's state of health and she had replied, he got down to the real reason for his call.

"Looks like you're going to be staying down there a while longer. I've been thinking—maybe I'd better go ahead and take care of getting the house listed myself. Places in that high a price range aren't selling too fast now, you know."

Charlene noted the undertone of apology that was invariably in Paul's voice when he talked to her now. But alongside the apology was another emotion—determination. He might feel guilty for having left her for another woman, but he intended to get this divorce. Evidently he and Susan must still be wildly and passionately in love.

"I suppose you may as well," she said slowly. "You're right—I probably won't be coming back to Atlanta anytime soon. Why don't you just go ahead and list with whatever agency you prefer since you'll be taking care of everything. And do me a favor, will you? Give the post office Cappy's address and have them forward my mail." In her own voice she heard a detachment that surprised her. Paul and the house and Atlanta seemed far away at this moment and not foremost in her thoughts. Was she adjusting so soon to losing him?

"I'll be glad to do that," he assured her quickly, surprise mingling with relief, the latter probably due to her lack of resistance to putting the house up for sale. "Please give your grandfather my best, and I'll keep you posted on the house. You'll probably have to sign the listing contract, too. If so, I'll send it down special delivery."

After hanging up the phone, Charlene stood for a long moment, examining her own feelings. Judging from Paul's eagerness to sell the house, she wouldn't be surprised if there were a FOR SALE sign in front of it tomorrow. What if it sold more quickly than he expected? When she did return to Atlanta, she wouldn't have a home to go back to. Aside from the practical considerations, Paul's decision to sell the house made the break between him and herself seem more real than it ever had before, more irremediable.

She had been fooling herself, hadn't she? There was little chance that the two of them would ever get back together now and work out their problems. Time and again she had seen couples separate and get back together again, but in few cases did the reconciliation last. Even if Paul tired of Susan eventually, he probably would not want to live with Charlene again, and for the first time, she wasn't even sure she would be willing to take him back. This last realization came as a decided shock.

Don't be a fool! she told herself with a little mental shake. *Of course you'd take him back!* In a few weeks Cappy would be back to normal and take over running the marina. Without the novelty of sharing that responsibility with Burt, she'd probably be bored to tears hanging around here. In no time at all, she would be wanting a good bridge game or a challenging tennis match. As Paul's wife, she'd enjoyed the best life had to offer. Of course, she'd take him back.

In the meantime, she had to get dressed and visit Cappy in the hospital. It was simply killing him that he wouldn't be here in the marina this weekend, where all the action involving the Mardi Gras Boat Parade would be going on.

By noon the next day, there hardly seemed room for another automobile in the marina. It appeared that every boat owner had invited at least two carloads of friends to come down and help decorate for the parade and drink beer and have a good time.

Burt was kept busy at the fuel dock while Charlene tended the store. Cappy's fuel dock was the only one on the river and boats from other marinas also came to top off their fuel tanks. Theoretically the members of the Krewe of Tchefuncte were the only participants in the parade scheduled for tomorrow, but the river would be thronged with boats of every size and description. Sometimes it seemed there were as many revelers on the water as there were on the banks of the town of Madisonville, where people gathered to catch the gaudy beads and other types of "throws" the costumed boat crews would toss, in true Mardi Gras tradition.

"Looks like it's going to be another gorgeous day!" Charlene predicted happily on Sunday morning when she and Burt were opening up. He produced a low grunt that matched the total lack of enthusiasm on his face. Charlene started to tease him about being a grump and then decided against it. The marina had been especially noisy last night with all the partying going on into the early hours of the morning. At midnight someone had initiated a contest of boat horns that awakened her with the loud blasts. Burt probably hadn't been able to sleep very well. Besides that, she knew he wasn't a morning conversationalist anyway.

Growing up in this area of Louisiana as she had, she was completely familiar with the tradition of Mardi Gras or "Fat Tuesday," a day of celebration and excess before Ash Wednesday, which signaled the beginning of the Lenten season of fasting. In reality the celebration began weeks before the actual day of Mardi Gras, and this year the weather had been balmy and springlike for most of that time. The Krewe of Tchefuncte couldn't possibly have asked for a better day for their parade. The sun shone brightly and the temperature ventured up to seventy degrees.

Charlene enjoyed every minute of the hectic day. She sold beer and ice and potato chips and Popsicles and laughed and joked with everybody who came into the store. They spilled in from both entrances, some from boats that had pulled up to the fuel dock.

By early afternoon there was a lull as everyone, either by boat or car, went to Madisonville, the actual location of the parade. Charlene sat on the fuel dock next to Burt and waved at the costumed boat crews as they floated by. The theme this year was Disneyland, and some of the boats were cunningly decorated to look like floating castles. Several larger boats had bands aboard, and strains of Dixieland music and rock and roll blared out over the water, as if in good-natured competition. Unconsciously she expelled a little sigh as the last boat disappeared around the bend of the river.

"You'd like to be on one of those boats yourself, wouldn't you? Yelling and throwing beads to the crowd in town?" Burt observed, his tone not exactly critical while it did suggest he couldn't understand *anyone* actually wanting to be part of a parade.

Charlene turned her head and let her eyes meet his, feeling defensive in spite of herself.

"What's wrong with wanting to have a good time?" she demanded. "Not everybody's a recluse and wants to be alone all the time like *you* do." Grimacing as she heard how aggressive she had sounded, she continued in a more moderate tone, "Some people just happen to be more sociable than others, I guess. I don't mind admitting that I do enjoy being around people. If that makes me superficial . . ." She lifted her shoulders in a philosophical shrug. And then against her better judgment, she just couldn't resist elaborating in the hope that she could open Burt's mind up to the narrowness of his life-style.

"Everybody needs a balance between work and play in their lives . . . between having a good time and taking things seriously. Don't you agree?"

He didn't look as if he did. His blue eyes were regarding her steadily, but his expression was thoughtfully distant. Probably he was thinking she had a lot of nerve lecturing him about how he should live his life, and he was right, of course!

"I guess you're wondering where I got my degree in philosophy!" she quipped, deciding the best thing was just to treat her little *spiel* as a joke. "As the old saying goes, it takes all kinds of people to make up the world. Some people like to ride in the parade and some would rather just watch." She glanced down at her wrist. "And speaking of *watch,* it's late and I'm starving. Why don't I make us some sandwiches since we both skipped lunch in the line of duty?"

He stood up, his eyes fixed on the swamp across the river so that she couldn't see their expression to try to gauge his mood.

"Thanks, but while it's quiet I think I'll go down and check my boat. You never know what some of these yahoos will take it into their heads to do. They don't seem to realize you don't just barge aboard somebody's boat any more than you would walk uninvited into somebody's house."

"I could wait until you get back to make lunch,"

Charlene offered. "We shouldn't be too busy for the rest of the afternoon now. Most of the action will be over in town."

She didn't have to explain to him, since he had grown up in Madisonville, that after the boats paraded along the banks of the town they would tie up at the public dock. The side streets would be blocked off from automobile traffic and there would be bands playing for dancing. The several local bars on the river would do a booming business.

"No, don't wait on me. I'll just grab a bite while I'm down on the boat."

Charlene got to her feet, knowing there was no changing his mind. Whatever his reasons, he chose not to eat lunch with her. Perhaps he was genuinely concerned about the welfare of his boat or perhaps he just wanted to be alone. Given his temperament, the last two days couldn't have been easy for him.

"Okay," she agreed. And then, wanting to compensate for any criticism he might have read into her comments prior to the lunch invitation, she added, "Why don't you just take the rest of the day off? I can handle things here. It shouldn't be that busy."

"I'll be back in an hour or so," he said, as if he hadn't even heard her offer.

"See you later then," she said, once again knowing there was little point in arguing with him. She had almost reached the steps leading up to the house when his voice stopped her.

"Charly."

Something in the tone warned her he had recalled a detail he needed to tell her. There was a strange premonitory tingling along her neck as she turned around and looked back at him.

"Yes?"

"You know you can't divide all the people in the world up into two neat, little groups, the ones riding in the parade and the ones on the sidelines watching it. There are always a few people who wouldn't walk half a block to see any kind of parade."

The odd mixture of amusement and gravity in his tone and in the blue eyes steadily regarding her left little doubt that he had read her motives earlier when she had expounded upon having a reasonable balance in one's life between fun and seriousness. He was telling her he knew she thought he was antisocial, and she would have to accept him as what he was or not at all.

"You're right, Burt," she said contritely and then turned and slowly climbed the steps, pondering what he had said. In one way, she knew he *was* right. No one had the right to try to change someone else's personality, and she shouldn't keep trying to change Burt's. But he had so many character traits that stirred her to the deepest kind of admiration that she just couldn't stand the thought of how he was limiting his life living the way he did. Couldn't he see how much he was missing?

By the time she had prepared and eaten her solitary lunch, Charlene had formed the resolution to heed Burt's request or ultimatum or whatever it had been. In the future, she would do or say nothing to encroach upon his sense of privacy or to challenge his life-style. Considering all he had done for her and

Cappy the last two weeks, it was the least she could do in return. Besides, there was little chance that Burt would ever change anyway.

He was later in returning than he had given her reason to expect. She had almost begun to think he had decided to take the rest of the day off after all when he finally appeared.

"Was everything all right at your boat?" she asked concernedly.

"Fine," he said, nodding his satisfaction. "Nobody was around at all so I drove over to Mandeville to pick up a few groceries. You're invited to dinner tonight if you want to brave my cooking."

Charlene struggled to hide her astonishment. The invitation was totally unexpected, especially after he had declined her own earlier today. And he hadn't invited her aboard his boat since that first day.

"I accept with pleasure," she declared. Remembering his easy familiarity with the galley that day he had made tea for the two of them, she expected him to be a more than competent cook.

"If you don't mind eating late, I thought we would visit Cappy first," he suggested casually. "I'll bet he has driven the whole hospital staff up the walls today."

She agreed, smiling in response to his amused grin and privately marveling at the way her spirits soared in anticipation of the evening ahead. It was such a relief to have Burt return in this light-hearted mood, obviously bearing her no hard feelings for their little exchange that afternoon. His friendship meant a lot to her.

That evening by the time they got back to the marina from visiting Cappy, nearly all the cars had gone and the atmosphere was quiet and peaceful. Charlene saw the satisfied smile on Burt's face as he got out of his car and glanced around. The smile broadened and took on an element of sheepishness as he caught her looking at him.

Down inside his boat, she lounged back comfortably and sipped a glass of white wine while he prepared an excellent meal: lamb chops with mint-flavored Bartlett pears, fresh cauliflower with cheese sauce, and a green salad of romaine lettuce and artichoke hearts.

"This looks like a celebration!" Charlene declared gaily when he uncorked a bottle of champagne. "Candlelight and champagne!" She smiled appreciatively at the tall taper in its brass candle holder.

"Why not?" he said, picking up his glass and clinking it against hers. "I think we've done a damned good job of pinch-hitting for Cappy, don't you? Trouble is we don't dare tell *him* that."

Charlene laughed delightedly.

"Heavens, no! It would hurt his feelings to think we managed to get along without him. He'd rather think the place is in shambles!" She sipped her champagne happily, enjoying the mood of camaraderie.

They both were hungry and attacked the food with enthusiasm.

"Burt, you're a great cook," she praised when she had finished, her empty plate convincing proof of her sincerity.

He refilled her champagne glass and she sat back, sipping champagne and feeling her mood grow more expansive.

"The two of us *have* done a good job of running this place, haven't we?" she demanded, the question an entirely rhetorical one. "I'm proud of us. Maybe when Cappy gets out of the hospital and sees that we can take care of things, he'll just relax and take it easy." She wanted to say more, much more, but curbed the impulse for the time being. With a little pushing and nudging from her, she hoped for a course of events that would work out well for all of them, Cappy and Burt and herself. Cappy was getting older and could use someone to work for him. Burt didn't seem to have any kind of commitments. There wasn't any reason he couldn't just stay here in the marina indefinitely. He must have to earn some money from time to time.

"I wouldn't raise my hopes about Cappy sitting back and letting somebody else run things in this marina," Burt warned, startling Charlene for a moment until she realized he was replying to the words she had spoken aloud and wasn't really reading her mind. "We'll be lucky if we can hold him back for a week or two."

"I guess you're right," she agreed, watching Burt as he picked up their plates and took them over to the counter. She didn't offer to help. He'd made it clear earlier that there was room for only one person to work in a galley that size.

"At least you'll be here to give him a hand," she

suggested. "He'll probably come closer to listening to you than to anybody else, including his doctor."

"I'll be here until he gets back on his feet. Then I'll be heading back for Florida. I hadn't planned on staying this long," he announced, coming back over to the table and continuing to clear it.

Charlene stared at him in open dismay.

"You're going *back* to Florida? Why, I thought you would probably stay . . ." She flushed as his eyebrows shot up in reaction to the sharp grievance in her tone. "It's your business if you want to go back there," she added hastily. "I just assumed . . . since your family all live here in this area and you've always been so fond of Cappy . . ." She picked up her champagne glass and sipped from it, knowing that she was making a fool of herself reacting like this, as if Burt didn't have every right to live wherever he chose. The news that he would be leaving Madisonville—and soon—had just come as a shock. So far he hadn't mentioned a word to her that would lead her to think he had serious ties in Florida, but perhaps he did. Maybe there was even a woman . . .

"What about you? How long are you planning to be here?" Burt inquired, breaking into her frowning speculation.

She thought about the question a moment. Her initial plan had been to stay only a week or two and then go back to Atlanta, but now she just didn't know what she would do. Paul had the house up for sale, and now that they would be getting a divorce, she wasn't sure she even wanted to continue to live in Atlanta. There was no special reason to do so.

"I don't know how long I'll stay," she said honestly. "As long as Cappy needs me, I guess—and maybe even after that. Maybe indefinitely."

"Who're you kidding, Charly?" Burt scoffed, the expression on his face deeply skeptical. "Your intentions might be the best, but how long will you be content living with Cappy here in the marina? This isn't your kind of life. The novelty is going to fade and you'll be missing your bridge games and tennis tournaments and fancy luncheons."

The fact that he was undoubtedly right didn't make her resent his astute observations any less.

"I didn't necessarily mean I would live *with* Cappy, in his house," she pointed out stiffly. "New Orleans offers all the advantages of a large city. There are lots of country clubs there—and some nice ones right around here, as far as that goes. I may buy a house or a condominium."

"I see," he said, going back into the galley area and busying himself rinsing the dishes and stacking them neatly beside the sink. Then he wiped the table with a wet sponge and put down the hinged leaves of the table.

Charlene's flare of resentment had all melted away by the time he had finished. She was poignantly aware that after tonight everything would be different for the two of them. Cappy would be coming home tomorrow, and she and Burt would no longer be in complete charge of the marina. As happy as she was to have Cappy recovering his health, she would still miss her partnership with Burt, even if her enjoyment had been based upon the novelty of her situation.

Suddenly it occurred to her that Burt had enjoyed the past two weeks working with her, too. She didn't know why she was so sure of that, but she was. Tonight *was* a kind of celebration. Why let thoughts of the future spoil it?

"Truce?" she pleaded softly when he came back to sit down.

He hesitated only a fraction of a heartbeat before sitting down next to her instead of opposite her as he had during their meal. Charlene let him take the wineglass out of her hand and set it on the narrow stationary portion of the table. She loved the way he combed his fingers slowly through the lustrous blackness of her hair as though the feel of the silken strands gave him great sensual pleasure. Lifting her own freed hands to his face, she traced his cheekbones and then the firm mouth she was already aching to have kiss her.

The mere prospect of his lovemaking had her aroused. Her breasts had grown heavier and rounder as though awaiting the touch of his hand. Her nipples were tingling and hardening prematurely, stimulated by her anticipation. Her entire body felt sensual and alive.

A wry smile deepened the corners of her mouth as she slipped her arms up around his neck and lifted her eyes to meet the somnolent blueness of his.

"What's funny?" he asked curiously, stopping the combing movement of his hands.

Charlene sighed luxuriously, took a quick little taste of his mouth, enjoying the cool firmness.

"What's funny is *me*," she murmured, unable to resist taking another quick, clinging kiss. This time his lips weren't quite so passive. "I'm not exactly 'hard to get' when we make love, am I?" She grazed her lips along the hard line of his jaw and felt him shiver, but he was listening carefully. His hands had dropped down now to loosely clasp her waist. "It really surprises me that I've turned into such a passionate woman. Sometimes I'm almost worried . . ."

She didn't get to complete the thought because Burt's hands had tightened at her waist and he was the one kissing her now and not teasingly as she had kissed him. Evidently he had received explanation enough of her mirth. As the kiss hardened and deepened, with his tongue searching for hers and finding it, Charlene found herself worrying about nothing, thinking about nothing. She relinquished herself totally to the sheer sensory joy of making love with him. With her limited experience, she lacked the qualifications to rank Burt in terms of his sexual expertise even if she had wanted to. All she knew was that he was a wonderful lover to her. Each time they made love, the experience seemed more intensely pleasurable than the last time.

Tonight she discovered the additional stimulation of telling him of the way she felt. Her own boldness added an edge of excitement.

"Did you know I love to touch your body?" she murmured as she unbuttoned his shirt and slipped it off his arms. To prove her point, she ran her palms along the muscled ridges of his shoulders, down his arms and across his stomach and up the hard contours of his chest. The quick intake of his breath and the blue fire blazing up in his eyes delighted her, and she laughed, compelled to tell him more. "I like to touch you, not just because of the way you feel to me, but because I can tell *you* really like it, too."

"You know what I *don't* like?" he asked gravely.

"What?" Charlene replied uncertainly. "Me talking so much . . . or being too forward?"

"Not that." He shook his head, his expression still disconcertingly serious. "I hate having to stop long enough to make more comfortable arrangements, but I don't want to make love to you on this narrow settee."

On the last few words he was grinning, and only then did Charlene realize he was teasing her. In mock anger she shoved him backward on the settee. He didn't resist, but instead reached up and pulled her down on top of him, his arms closing around her so tight she couldn't budge. With her face lifted a few inches above his, she saw the raw passion in his eyes and features, felt it in the tumescence of his maleness thrust against her pelvis.

"Oh, Burt . . ." she began, overwhelmed by that compulsion to talk again, but then lowered her lips to his instead, finding them hungry and responsive. There seemed no end to the kiss, the almost savage meshing of their mouths together, the urgent union of their tongues. But finally she was afraid his heart would burst against her breast, its pounding was so wild and deafening, and she dragged her lips apart from his, her breathing coming in gasps.

He sat up, bringing her up with him, and turned her around so that she sat on his lap. His fingers dealt with the buttons of her blouse, and in short time he had removed the blouse and then her bra. Charlene breathed in, thrusting her breasts forward as he bent and kissed each one of them. He said nothing, but she *knew* he felt exactly as she had felt earlier when she was caressing his body. His pleasure was a combination of pure selfish sensation and awareness of the stimulation he aroused in her with his touch. As she thrust her fingers into his hair and massaged the hardness of his bone structure, his teeth closed gently on a nipple, and she moaned aloud, pulling his head convulsively against her breast.

One of his hands had been sliding up and down the inside of her thigh. Now it made a devastatingly intimate stroking motion that brought his name bursting from her lips in a tone that held entreaty. The wayward hand stopped and he lifted his head from her breasts. She met the inquiry in his eyes and then looked around the cabin interior with a bewildered expression.

"Where . . . ?" she blurted awkwardly. He had said something about more "comfortable arrangements."

Humor brightened the understanding that flashed into his eyes. He lifted her by her waist and set her feet on the floor. She watched as he deftly performed a feat of magic. Suddenly the high narrow berth behind the settee became a wide bunk. The settee cushion formed part of the mattress.

"How clever!" she exclaimed but her eyes were drawn back to Burt, and they wandered over his smooth, naked torso. Her hands itched to touch him again, to finish undressing him. He still wore his jeans as did she. Her eyes asked his permission as she took a step closer and reached a little uncertainly toward his waistband. His lids drooped in a silent affirmative as he read her intention and stood there watching her as she broke open the heavy snap and slid down the zipper.

With conscious and deliberate provocation, she pulled down the heavy denim jeans and removed them, then his cotton briefs. Her boldness stoked her own desire even as it raised his to an urgency that made him much quicker than she had been when he finished undressing her.

"Tease," he accused huskily, picking her up and holding her tight against him when they both were naked.

Charlene tightened her arms around his neck, reveling in their closeness with no separating barriers of clothing.

"Why do you call me that?" she demanded, kissing his neck and then nipping him gently with her teeth. "A tease promises what she isn't willing to deliver." The seductive cadences of her voice challenged him to test out her promise. And he did.

Afterwards, Charlene lay for long moments beside him on the broad bunk, utterly spent and bemused as she considered the abandon of their lovemaking tonight. Neither of them had held back anything this time. It had truly been an experience beyond words, but she hadn't been able to hold them back in the height of her passion.

"Aren't you sorry now you accused me of being a tease?" she asked drowsily, snuggling closer to him. She felt warm and content and sleepy.

"Maybe I should have said *sorceress.*"

She hadn't really been expecting an answer, and certainly not this one spoken in a reflective, serious tone. Charlene didn't find the speculation in the least flattering.

"You mean like Circe, the famous Greek witch your boat is named after?" she asked skeptically. When he didn't reply at once, she took the silence as an affirmative answer and her sense of injury mounted. "I would never turn men into pigs!" she declared emphatically.

"But you enjoy wielding power over men, don't you? All women do."

He sounded so completely objective, as if he were merely stating a universally accepted truth and not being personally offensive, that Charlene was at a loss as to how to answer him. She supposed it *was* true that women enjoyed exerting their feminine influence over men, but then men had ways of controlling women, too. It worked both ways. She had every intention of pursuing the subject, but before she could decide what to say next, Burt was sitting up and then swinging down to the floor. She watched him pull on his clothes, comprehension taking shape in her head.

"You don't want me to sleep with you, do you?" she blurted when it was fully formed. Surprise made her risk trampling on forbidden territory. Just that afternoon she had sworn to herself not to threaten Burt's sense of privacy, no matter how little she understood it, and yet here she was making an issue of what puzzled her no end. He had never really "slept" with her. For some reason, she had thought the power of their lovemaking tonight might make a difference.

"I don't think it would be a good idea for you to stay all night on the boat," he said reasonably. "Somebody is bound to notice and start some gossip. It would be awkward for Cappy. You know how straight-laced he is. My parents are, too."

Charlene didn't argue, recognizing the explanation as altogether irrefutable, but she wasn't buying it for a moment. Now she understood why he wasn't letting himself be lured into sleeping with her. He took his mythology seriously. He wasn't taking any chances of letting down his guard with women, not even in his sleep.

"Did you name your boat yourself or was it already called *Circe* when you bought it?" she asked offhandedly as she tucked her blouse into her jeans.

He looked surprised at the question.

"It's bad luck to change the name of a boat. She was already named *Circe*. Why do you ask?"

"Just curious," she replied evasively, deciding to let the whole subject drop. Hadn't she learned her lesson that afternoon? Burt wasn't ever going to change his views of women any more than he was going to become gregarious. More than once he'd tried to tell her he was the way he was and she could take him like that or not at all.

To make matters even more delicate, she had played a part herself in disillusioning him about women. She was inclined now to forget entirely about that incident in her youth twelve years ago, but somehow she doubted Burt ever forgot it. Not for a moment. Not even when they made love.

Chapter Six

Charlene had chosen to go to a doctor across the lake in Metairie out of discretion. Now she was glad that she had, for more reasons than one. The thirty-minute drive across the Lake Pontchartrain Causeway would give her time to ponder the incredible news she had learned: SHE WAS PREGNANT!

"But I can't be pregnant!" she had argued with the doctor when she returned to his office this afternoon to get the result of the morning's test. "My husband and I have been trying for five years!"

Dr. Laver had eyed his patient with a mixture of impatience and skepticism. If she was already so convinced she couldn't be pregnant, why had she come to him in the first place? his expression said.

"You are pregnant, Mrs. Reed," he said firmly. "You'll want to get in touch with your regular gynecologist in Atlanta as soon as you return. This prescription will help alleviate your morning sickness, which according to what you've told me is rather severe. In the meantime, if you have any problems . . ."

A dazed Charlene took her cue and left. As the truth gradually sank in, an incredible feeling of joy welled up inside her, like helium inflating a human-sized balloon. If it hadn't been for the roof of her car, she might have just floated home across Lake Pontchartrain.

She was going to have a baby!

It came as an overwhelming surprise that she was so elated over the discovery, which she hadn't suspected would bring this kind of excitement and joy. She must be crazy to feel happy over being pregnant at this particular time of her life. Here she was, thirty years old and about to get a divorce from her husband, who wasn't even the father of the child anyway! And yet, she couldn't stop smiling. The other drivers on the causeway probably thought she was some kind of loony, driving along all by herself grinning from ear to ear!

What was she going to do? Since the baby wasn't Paul's, she couldn't expect him to assume any responsibility for it, nor did she want him to. It was *her* baby! She would take care of it herself. Suddenly her life held a purpose and meaning it had never had before.

Not for a moment did she give more than passing consideration to telling Burt the truth, for what constructive purpose would it serve for him to know? Before long, he would be leaving Madison-ville, going back to Florida, where he would contin-ue to live his aimless, carefree life, carefully avoiding human entanglements. To know he had a child somewhere might threaten the peace of mind he valued above all else. Besides which, Charlene ad-mitted with complete honesty, she didn't really want to share the baby. It was hers and hers alone. Only she would know the secret of its father's identity.

There were practical reasons to tell Cappy her news, aside from the suspicion that she might burst if she didn't share it with another person. Even if the prescription the doctor had written for her did alleviate the devastating morning sickness, she still wasn't likely to be her normal, bouncy self in the mornings. Cappy might worry needlessly about her and he might also say something to arouse Burt's suspicions.

She broke the news to Cappy that same night, having to suppress the sharp twinges of conscience when she allowed him to jump to the obvious conclusion that the baby was Paul's. Thanks mainly to Burt's discretion, Cappy apparently hadn't any suspicion that she and Burt had been having an affair.

"Do me a favor, Cappy," she requested. "Don't mention anything about this to anybody for a while. It's kind of awkward . . . the divorce and all."

He nodded in agreement.

"Maybe now there won't be no divorce," he suggested hopefully.

Her reply was carefully noncommittal. Mentally

she was examining her own feelings with considerable interest. No longer did she have any inclination to try to salvage her marriage. That had been one phase of her life. Now she was entering another.

"Don't look so melancholy, Cappy!" she chided, emerging from her self-absorption and noting his pensive expression. "You're going to be a great-grandfather! Doesn't *that* make you feel ancient? Remember that you're always telling me things have a way of working out for the best," she cajoled, trying to lighten his mood.

"Sure they do," he agreed, drawing on his pipe and nodding slowly. "Always people arrivin' in the world and other people leavin'." His sigh came from deep within his chest.

Charlene winced at the stabbing pain inside her own chest. She knew what he was going to say even before he continued, and her heart ached for him.

"Burt told me today he'll be headin' back to Florida pretty soon now. I was sure hopin' he would decide to stay," Cappy said heavily.

"I know you were, Cappy," she said gently. "But it wouldn't be fair to make Burt feel bad about wanting to lead his own kind of life, would it? His being here to help out when we needed him was a godsend. He must figure you're well enough now to take over things yourself." Her last comment was a deliberate bait to rouse him and get his mind off its sad reflections.

"Durn right, I'm well," he declared strongly, snorting his disgust that anyone would believe the contrary. "Two weeks in that dad-burned hospital and now three weeks of sittin' around here with you and Burt telling me not to do this and not to do that every time I lift a hand!" He got up and bade her a gruff good night and stomped off to bed.

Charlene got up and switched off the television and turned out all the lights. Sitting in the darkness, she thought about the pure wonder of knowing she had a human life growing inside her. Nothing could diminish her joy over that knowledge, but Burt's leaving and her grandfather's sadness gave that joy a bittersweetness. For the first time, she admitted to herself that she, too, was going to miss Burt a great deal when he was gone. But if he *had* to leave, it was better that he go soon before she and Cappy became any more dependent upon him than they already were, before he learned her secret.

What was he doing tonight? Most likely he was alone on his boat, listening to music, reading, thinking. What would his reaction be if he knew of the bond that had been forged between him and herself? Perhaps she was making a mistake by not telling him, but looking at matters from every possible angle, she kept concluding that he was better off *not* knowing.

During the days that followed, Charlene imagined that she moved about encircled by a bright nimbus her inner happiness generated. On her lips a smile lingered and her dark eyes glowed with a secret elation. More than once she would look around and catch Burt staring at her intently, obviously puzzled over the reason for her constant good mood, but he never questioned her outright. It wasn't his way.

One day she overheard a snatch of conversation between him and Cappy.

"Charly sure seems in high spirits these days," Burt commented.

Charlene held her breath, waiting for Cappy's reply. Was he going to confide in Burt that she was pregnant?

"Looks like she might be gettin' back together with Paul," Cappy answered after a slight pause.

Now Charlene strained to hear whatever Burt's reaction to that information would be, but he said nothing further to give her a clue. Probably it mattered not to him one way or another, except that he would be glad of anything that made Cappy feel good.

Following that exchange, Burt never touched her again and perhaps it was just accident or chance, but he was never alone in her company. She missed his companionship, but she was totally absorbed in what was taking place in her body. And then, with no fanfare or fuss, he was gone. The night before his departure he ate dinner with her and Cappy, told them good-bye in the most offhanded kind of manner, and was gone before dawn the following morning.

Cappy's eyes were suspiciously bright when he came into the house for lunch that day. Charlene had shed some tears herself and suffered some self-doubts. Had she been wrong not to tell Burt she carried his child? *But what good would it have done for him to know?* she kept asking herself. He was a loner. There wasn't any possibility that she would marry him and share his kind of life, especially not with a child.

"The old saying 'you can't go home again' was true in Burt's case," she said quietly, pouring Cappy a glass of iced tea and sitting at the table with him. "We're both going to miss him a lot for a while."

"No doubt about that," he agreed, showing little interest in his sandwich. "It's my own fool fault for raisin' my hopes. Burt told me he'd be here just long enough to get this place rebuilt, and then he ended up stayin' longer when I had that second attack."

Charlene was looking at him in surprise.

"You mean Burt came here especially to oversee the work you had done in the marina?" she inquired curiously.

"Not just oversee it." Cappy took a bite of his sandwich and chewed it, washing it down with iced tea. He eyed the growing puzzlement evident on her face and shrugged. "Reckon there ain't much reason to keep it secret anymore. Burt was the one who put up the money for the new pilings and docks. He didn't want anybody to know about it, 'specially his folks. He didn't want them thinkin' he'd moved back here for good."

"But where did he get that kind of money?" she exclaimed.

Cappy looked as though the question was a silly one.

"Mean you didn't know he has a big boatyard business in Florida? I figured you would put two and two together yourself and figure out who my 'silent partner' was."

Charlene was busy with her thoughts. She had put two and two together right at first, but had come up with the wrong answer, mainly because nobody had ever given her a hint that Burt had a business in Florida. Cappy might have assumed that she already knew it, but Burt had deliberately let her believe he was just a drifter, going from place to place on his boat, working just enough to survive. Why hadn't he told her the truth?

She puzzled over that question throughout the day, and the only answer that seemed logical only reinforced her assurance that she had done the right thing in not telling Burt about her pregnancy. Perhaps he was afraid she was one of those divorcées on the loose and didn't want her to think he was eligible.

Before many days had passed, she put the whole matter out of her mind. The inner clock that had always kept her moving at a frenetic pace slowed, and she found herself utterly content, living with Cappy in the marina, helping him tend the store on weekends when there was traffic on the river, sharing with him the housekeeping and cooking chores. After a while he stopped asking her if she had told Paul about the baby.

Amazingly, she hadn't. Every time she had tried, she just hadn't been successful. "Paul, there's something important we have to talk about," she would begin whenever he gave her an opening, having called for some specific reason concerning the divorce. Alarmed at the tone of her voice, perhaps, he would suddenly find himself in an urgent hurry to terminate the conversation, pleading that he had an appointment or was expecting an important call.

It occurred to Charlene finally that he evidently was fearful of some attempts on her part to postpone or halt the divorce procedure. If she hadn't been so serenely complacent, she might have become irritated and just blurted the news out to him, but she really didn't see that it concerned him anyway. After a while she halfway forgot that he didn't know, and the telephone conversations weren't frequent anyway.

In mid-June when he called with the jubilant news that the house was sold, she was in her fourth month of pregnancy and proud of her swelling abdomen.

"Why, that's good news," she said pleasantly. "I suppose I'll have to come to Atlanta for the act of sale."

He told her it was scheduled for the first part of July. If she was agreeable, they could even meet together with their respective lawyers at that time and settle the property. The separation period in both Georgia and Louisiana was one year. Next January, they would be eligible for divorce.

Charlene would be happy to get everything completed in one trip to Atlanta and then she wouldn't have to go back.

"I'll see if I can get an early-morning flight into Atlanta on the fourteenth," she said, thinking that the timing of the house sale had worked out well. Before long, she wouldn't want to be traveling.

"You're going to *fly?*" he asked, surprised. "I thought you would drive . . . visit old friends and all that." His voice changed midway as though he were reminding himself it was none of his business what she chose to do.

It occurred to her Paul still didn't know she was pregnant and she tried once again to tell him, only to have him break in and suggest they wait until she got to Atlanta to discuss whatever it was that she thought so important.

"I'm supposed to be meeting Susan in about ten minutes," he said nervously.

Charlene didn't persist. He would find out soon enough, and it would be his own fault he had no forewarning.

Four weeks later when her flight arrived in Atlanta, Paul was waiting for her at the gate. He had arranged for them to go directly from the airport to an attorney's office for the act of sale on their home.

Charlene was wearing a red maternity pantsuit, and she knew she looked radiant, as she had been told in the New Orleans airport and again on the plane. By now she had grown accustomed to total strangers telling her how lovely she looked. The young man who had sat beside her on the plane insisted upon carrying her small suitcase, and in the process of thanking him and bidding him good-bye, she didn't even notice Paul at first.

"My God!" came a strangled exclamation, and she looked around to see him staring at her as though she were a hideous specter. "You're *pregnant!"* he whispered, his voice horrified.

"I'm sorry, Paul," she apologized contritely, noting with compassion how pale he had gone. "I kept trying to tell you over the telephone, but you just never would let me get it out. I guess I should have mailed you a card," she joked ruefully.

He might not even have heard her.

"You should have *told* me," he said weakly, wiping a hand across his forehead. "I don't understand what you were thinking about—the house is sold now—the divorce is going through . . ." He stopped, shaking his head as if trying to clear away the confusion.

"But you don't understand!" Charlene began, realizing that he thought the baby was his. "Please, let me explain—"

She let him lead her over to a chair and when they were both seated, she met his eyes squarely. Determined to set him straight, she was thus not as tactful as she might have been.

"It's not your baby, Paul," she stated with blunt emphasis. "It has nothing to do with you, so just relax. I intend to take full responsibility for my child myself."

"Not *my* baby?" he echoed in disbelief. "Well, whose *is* it then?"

Charlene had to blink she was so amazed at his tone of voice. He acted positively outraged, as though he were a wronged husband!

"That's really not your concern," she said firmly and then glanced down at her wristwatch. "Hadn't we better get going? We don't want to be late."

He shot up out of the seat without another word and accompanied her in grim silence through the long concourse and eventually out to the parking lot, where Charlene saw that he had a brand-new Mercedes. Trying to return matters to normal, she complimented him on it, but to no avail. He maintained a stony silence for several more minutes, breaking it only when they were in the thick of traffic.

"I intend to fight you, you know," he bit out harshly, causing her to jump. "I have no intention of paying child support for somebody else's kid." He jerked his head sideways and glared at her.

Charlene's sympathy dissipated abruptly.

"If you'd just listen to me instead of being so bullheaded, you'd know I don't *want* you to pay child support. I told you I intend to take care of the baby myself," she said impatiently.

He gave her another of those sidelong stares.

"Will you put that in writing?" he rejoined tersely.

"Yes, I'll put it in writing," she agreed wearily.

Privately she was thinking it was a damned shame her last dealings with Paul had to be so unpleasant. She had wondered what she would feel at seeing him again after an absence of more than five months. So far he hadn't said or done anything to make her feel nostalgic.

"I'll have my attorney draw up a legal statement. That way I won't have you coming back later and trying to claim support for this kid. You'll have to name the real father, too," he said grimly.

"Okay. Okay. Whatever will ease your mind," Charlene agreed resignedly, wanting to put the subject to rest.

That evening she found herself totally exhausted from the strain of what had turned out to be a long day. Paul could scarcely have been more unpleasant if he had tried. He seemed to take it as a personal affront that she had gotten herself pregnant with another man's child. The implication was that she just hadn't *tried* hard enough to become pregnant with his child when they were living as husband and wife!

Perhaps their marriage would not have failed if she had succeeded in bearing him a child, but the whole question was futile now. All she wanted was to finish up her business here in Atlanta and get back to Cappy and the marina as fast as possible. There she could bask, like a contented cat, in the contemplation of the birth of her child. She didn't like bringing her unborn baby into the midst of all this conflict and discord.

"Oh, no, *please!*" she groaned aloud when the telephone rang about nine o'clock. She had just returned to her room after eating dinner in the hotel restaurant, intending to lie back on the bed and watch television for a while before going to sleep. The caller must be Paul, no doubt about to deliver a new brand of torment.

"Yes," she said tiredly into the receiver.

"Hello, Charly. This is Burt Landry," came a terse, familiar voice over the line.

"Burt!" she echoed, stunned. Why was he calling her here in Atlanta? How on earth had he even learned of her whereabouts? Unreasoning panic gripped her as she thought of the only plausible

explanation. "Has something happened to Cappy?" she asked sharply, sitting up in bed and clutching her abdomen with her free hand.

"No, nothing's wrong with Cappy. I talked to him on the telephone just a few minutes ago."

"I see," she said vaguely, not really seeing at all. "If nothing's wrong with Cappy, then why are you calling me?" And then another possibility dawned, one that curdled her blood. She waited apprehensively for his answer.

"Your husband, Paul Reed, called me tonight with some information I'd like you to verify personally. Is it true you're pregnant—with *my* child?"

Charlene winced at the tone of his voice. He had himself under control, but he was furious. Dear God, what a mess this was! First, she'd had to contend with Paul's sense of injury and now Burt's. Didn't these men understand that she expected *nothing* from them?

"He had no right to call you!" she said exasperatedly, leaning back against the pillows stacked behind her and closing her eyes wearily. "He's just so damned scared somebody might expect him to pay child support—"

"I don't care about that," Burt broke in icily. "You haven't answered my question. Is it my baby?"

Charlene didn't like his wording on that last question, and she was more than a little fed up with trying to be considerate of other people's feelings.

"It's *my* baby," she corrected testily. "Damn it, I wish everybody would just get that straight."

The silence on the line was unrelenting. He was still waiting for her to answer his question.

"You are the father, technically speaking," she admitted, choosing her words carefully. "But I'll sign a paper to clear you of responsibility, too, if that's what you want." Her voice was muffled with tears on that last. She was so tired of all this fuss over who was the father of her baby.

"Why in hell didn't you tell me before I left Madisonville? Cappy told me you knew you were pregnant then." He was still speaking in that tone of cold, contained fury.

Charlene sighed into the receiver. What a mess this was all developing into!

"Burt, I wish you hadn't called Cappy. I didn't want him to know any of this," she lamented. Then she forced her mind to concentrate on her reasons for not telling him. If she could, she would like to explain without hurting his feelings.

"I thought you were better off not knowing. That's all. What would you have done if I *had* told you? You obviously have no interest in settling down with a family. I didn't even know you had a business in Florida until after you'd gone. As far as I knew, you didn't work regularly. I didn't even know you were Cappy's silent partner. I think I had a right to know that." Her voice took on belligerence toward the last.

"You're absolutely sure it's *my* baby?" he asked brusquely, ignoring all the rest.

"Absolutely sure," she confirmed in a monotone. "Now if you don't mind, I don't feel like talking anymore tonight. It's been an unbelievably exhausting day. I'm sorry Paul called you. It definitely was not my idea. So *please*—just forget the whole thing."

"What do you plan to do?"

Something implacable in his voice sounded a warning to Charlene. He wasn't going to take her advice and dismiss from his mind the existence of a child who shared his genes. Damn Paul!

"I plan to take care of things here in Atlanta. That should take a few days. Then I'll fly back to New Orleans. Cappy must have mentioned that I plan to live with him, at least for the time being."

"He did tell me that," Burt said tersely. "Look—I think it would be best for me to fly to Atlanta, and then we can work out the best way to handle this. I should be able to get a flight sometime tonight."

"You come to Atlanta?" she exclaimed in dismay, forgetting how tired she was and sitting bolt upright. "But there's no reason for that! There's nothing to be *handled!* I'm having this baby and taking care of it myself! It's *mine!"*

The last words were muffled as tears began to course down her cheeks. She had had more than she could handle for one day.

"We'll talk about it when I get there." He said good-bye and hung up before she could muster the energy to make further efforts to dissuade him.

She lay back against the pillows and thought about this totally unforeseen development. What did Burt have in mind? Surely he didn't intend to marry her. If he had some hare-brained idea about asking for equal custody, he was crazy. She would never agree to that. He had no proof of paternity anyway. In any case, she was exhausted and needed her rest.

At a few minutes past seven the next morning, she was awakened by knocking on her door. Raising herself up groggily on one elbow, she wondered who could be bothering her at this hour. Surely Paul wasn't out there already! Getting out of bed, she walked up close to the door and called sleepily, "Who is it?"

"It's me, Burt," came the answer.

Then she remembered last night's telephone conversation. Without stopping to think that she wore nothing but her nightgown, whose pale pink nylon and lace revealed the swell of her abdomen and the new fullness of her breasts, she unlocked the door and opened it. She might have been self-conscious at the sharpness of his scrutiny if she hadn't been so taken aback by his own appearance. He wore a suit and tie! If she had met him at the airport, she might not have recognized him at first glance.

"That certainly was fast!" she murmured as he stepped past her, carrying a suitcase. "You can see for yourself I definitely am pregnant," she said in an attempt to dispel the heavy awkwardness. He was staring at her in much the same way Paul had yesterday, as if he couldn't believe what he saw.

"I'll order some coffee," she announced, going over to the telephone. When she had completed the call for room service and turned around, he stood in exactly the same place, still holding the suitcase.

"Would you like to sit down?" she offered, gesturing toward the corner of the room where two armchairs were placed on either side of a table.

"This takes some getting used to," he muttered, as if to himself. When he had set his suitcase down and dropped into one of the chairs, Charlene noted the fatigue in his eyes and face. He had probably been up all night.

"Excuse me while I wash my face," she said politely, slipping on a peignoir that matched her floor-length nightgown. When she returned from the bathroom, having washed her face and combed her hair, she felt ready to confront him. After a good night's sleep, she was no longer tired and easily discouraged the way she had been last night.

Perching on the edge of the bed in which she had slept, she smiled easily.

"Between you and Paul, I'm going to develop a complex," she said teasingly. "You two act as if you'd never seen a pregnant woman before!"

A shadow of a smile grazed his mouth.

"I've never seen a woman pregnant with *my* child before," he said soberly. "You look beautiful."

The totally unexpected compliment brought a lovely flush of pleasure to Charlene's face, enhancing her beauty.

"Thank you," she said simply. "I guess it's because I'm so happy, Burt. I didn't have any idea that being pregnant would be like this. It's wonderful!"

"Don't you mind?" His eyes dropped to her stomach.

She glanced down, too, giving herself a little pat.

"You mean losing my figure? I guess I may have some regrets afterwards, but I think it's worth it." She paused, a bemused expression on her face. "He just gave me a good kick!" she exclaimed softly. Then to counter the awkwardness when he kept staring at her so intently, she drew back her shoulders and thrust her breasts into greater prominence. "Besides—this is the first time in my life I've ever had big boobs!"

It came as something of a relief when the coffee was delivered. Burt seemed at a complete loss for words.

Sitting in the other chair, Charlene poured each of them a cup. Judging from what had transpired thus far, she hadn't changed her original opinion that Burt was wasting his time coming here to Atlanta. She took the opportunity now to give him her honest advice.

"Burt, now that you've seen for yourself I really *am* pregnant—and doing just *fine*—why don't you just go back to Florida and forget all this," she urged reasonably.

"I can't do that, Charly," he objected gravely. The promptness of his reply, as well as the tone, made her heart do a little quickstep of nervousness and then beat fast.

"What do you have in mind, then?" she asked with a note of impatience. The pause between them took on suspense for her as his gaze traveled intently over her bulky, sitting form before lifting to meet her eyes.

"I can't just *forget* about a human being that I'm

partly responsible for," he said almost hesitantly, as though he found it difficult to verbalize the feelings inside him.

Charlene wasn't really surprised at what he said. Her main reason for not telling him about the baby in the first place was not to destroy his peace of mind about something that had happened and couldn't be changed. Now Paul had blundered in and really muddied up the waters. What did Burt specifically have in mind, though? She had to tread so carefully in finding out because he wasn't a casual lover she had met on a vacation in Louisiana. He was a man she had spurned cruelly in her youth and then discovered twelve years later to be a really fine human being. To complicate matters more, he shared a deep bond of love with her grandfather.

"You mean you want to take financial responsibility?" she probed tactfully.

Resolution hardened all the planes of his face. The blue of his eyes was almost blinding in its brilliance, and she stared into them as though temporarily hypnotized.

"Not just that," he said firmly.

Charlene sucked in her breath and rose out of the chair in instinctive protest, pacing away from him as though dramatizing the threat he wielded. Whirling around, she clutched her swollen abdomen in a gesture symbolically protective of the life inside her.

"You can't have my baby!" she cried, fear inside her growing as she noted the hysteria in her voice. "I'm the *mother!* How on earth would you take care of a child! Maybe after it's older, in school . . ." Her voice waned when she saw that he wasn't listening. Staring down with intent concentration at the cup of coffee in his hands, he was blocking out her entreaties. In her desperation she changed swiftly to another tack.

"Come now, Burt," she said in a challenging voice, "you can't even prove this child *is* yours."

He looked up then and met her eyes directly. The implacable purpose she saw in his face made her suddenly so unsteady she had to back up several steps and sit on the edge of the nearest bed. Burt was impervious to both logic and emotion. He had made up his mind, and she didn't know if she would be able to sway him. Dear God, he wanted her child! For a horrible moment she had an image of the two of them pulling and tugging on a faceless infant. Shuddering, she spoke again, this time her tone one of weary capitulation.

"Forget I said that. Please. Of course, the child is yours . . . biologically. I would never deny that. But you're in no position to take care of a baby, not even six months out of the year. It wouldn't make sense to take a child away from its natural mother and put it in the care of a maid or a day-care center."

"I'm not suggesting that," he said, frowning and looking away from her at an angle. She could see the tenseness of his jawline. Had she unknowingly made him angry just now?

"What *are* you suggesting then?" she asked tentatively.

"You can come to Florida and have the baby. I'll take care of you both," he answered without any hesitation, his voice clipped and totally without expression.

Charlene studied his profile, still at a loss as to exactly what he was suggesting. It certainly didn't sound as if he were proposing marriage.

"Now let me see if I have this straight," she said warily. "You plan to take on the support of a pregnant woman who is in the process of getting a divorce from another man. What are your friends and employees in Florida going to think? What about Cappy? And your parents?" She didn't even mention explaining an unconventional arrangement to the baby some years down the line because that would have raised the subject of what she had intended to tell the child when he or she was old enough to ask about a father. In truth, she hadn't worked all that out in her mind yet.

Burt shrugged.

"They'll just have to realize I can't marry you until you have your divorce," he said in a tone that showed his impatience with regard to what other people thought of his actions.

"You plan to marry me!" Charlene blurted before she could catch the words back. Burt turned his head then and looked directly at her.

"Certainly I intend for my son or daughter to have my name," he said curtly.

Charlene realized then that he had come to Atlanta knowing his intention was to marry her. Why had he approached the matter in such a roundabout way? The answer was so painfully obvious. She had rejected him once before and was probably the last person in the world he would ever want to marry. God, what a mess! And she couldn't even give him a simple *yes* or *no*. There were considerations she knew hadn't occurred to him.

"There's so much more involved here than just giving a child a name, Burt," she pointed out urgently. "We have to think about your best interests . . . and mine, too," she said reluctantly. "If I remarry, I automatically forfeit Paul's alimony, which is a substantial amount of money. He's agreed to pay it for five years, during which time I am to prepare myself for earning a living. Living with Cappy, I could save most of that money. With it and the property settlement, I could take care of the baby and be independent."

It hadn't been easy to talk under the sharp cynicism of his gaze. Charlene knew he was thinking she hadn't changed. She was still mercenary to the core. Nevertheless, all these things needed to be said, and she continued doggedly.

"What if we *do* get married and then somewhere along the way, for whatever reason, one of us decides to get a divorce? You have no idea of what you're risking, Burt. The expense and the complication—believe me, right now I feel like an expert on the subject." She implored him with her eyes and her whole being to listen to what she was saying, but he looked totally unmoved as though he were just sitting there patiently until she was finished.

Summoning her courage with a deep intake of breath she came to the part that caused her the strongest reservations about his strange marriage proposal.

"Have you thought about how you'd be changing your whole life? What you'd be giving up? You're used to living alone. Can you adjust to having someone around you all the time, not just at your business, but when you come home as well?" she asked earnestly.

Some emotion flickered in the impenetrable blueness of his eyes, but it was quickly suppressed. Charlene let her shoulders sag and she waited quietly for him to speak. She had made her impassioned plea, for both their sakes. Now it was up to him.

"None of that changes the fact that I feel responsible," he said gravely. "You and I aren't the only people involved here. Besides the baby, there's Cappy to consider. He doesn't need any extra worry at this time of his life. What if you have complications with your pregnancy—have you thought of that?"

The contrite expression on Charlene's face said that she had thought of it.

"In another month or so, I won't be much help to him," she said ruefully, looking down at her stomach. Raising her eyes, she searched his face, looking in vain for some kind of reassurance she couldn't find. "Okay, Burt," she said almost wistfully. "If you're sure . . ."

"I'm sure," he returned without hesitation.

The grimness of his tone stirred an unexpected poignancy in her breast, and for a moment Charlene was on the verge of tears. What did she expect from

Burt, anyway? Certainly not some declaration of his affection. She was the same pragmatic woman who had told him in plain language some months ago her views of marriage. Now he was offering her just such a "convenient living arrangement," and she felt oddly disappointed. There was no time for the luxury of wallowing in emotion and no point in it, either.

"How long will your business keep you here in Atlanta?" Burt asked, rousing her to the immediate present.

"Another day or two, at least," she answered.

"I'll stay here until you're ready to leave. We can fly down to Florida together. In the meantime, I'll contact my cousin Ronnie in Madisonville. He can drive your car to Florida with your clothes and things from Cappy's."

Charlene could find no fault with these plans. At her stage of pregnancy, she would prefer not to make that long drive from Louisiana to Florida herself. It didn't surprise her that Burt had everything thought out in advance.

"Where are you going?" she blurted in surprise as he picked up his suitcase and headed for the door.

He stopped and looked around at her, his expression a little impatient as though his intentions should be obvious to her.

"I'm going to get a room," he explained. "This hotel will be as good as any other one since I'll have to stay somewhere until you're ready to leave."

"Why don't you stay here with me?" Charlene asked in amazement and then watched the play of expressions on his face. It hadn't even occurred to him that he could share a hotel room with her! To her, this was proof that he didn't know what he was getting himself into when he suggested marrying her.

"It's silly for you to pay for another room," she insisted, deciding to force the situation upon him as a kind of test. "We're not exactly strangers, and I'll be gone most of the day today. You can catch up on your sleep."

He was turning the idea over in his mind as though it were some bizarre object he found not in the least appealing.

"I wouldn't want to intrude upon your privacy," he said reluctantly, his eyes going to the two double beds, his mind evidently trying out the notion of sleeping in one of them.

Charlene took no pity on him. She stood up, a rueful smile twitching the corners of her mouth. The dusky pink of her long dressing gown enhanced her vivid brunette's coloring. She had never looked more beautiful in her life as she declared, "You might as well get used to the idea of living with a blimp. Now I have to get dressed and afterwards I intend to have a huge breakfast." The smile on her lips broadened with recollection. "You're lucky you missed the morning sickness phase."

With that she collected her underwear from the suitcase lying open across the room and went into the bathroom to take a shower. Burt couldn't expect her to take his marriage proposal seriously if he couldn't bear the prospect of sharing a hotel room with her for a couple of days.

When she came out of the bathroom and slipped into her maternity dress in the dressing alcove, a glance in the mirror told her Burt had decided to stay. He lay still dressed, but minus the jacket and tie, on the unslept-in bed. His head turned sideways and he watched her as she combed her hair and applied light makeup.

They ate breakfast together in the hotel restaurant. Afterwards Charlene took a taxi to her attorney's office, where she and Paul were to meet and continue the task of dividing up their long list of possessions. Before now, she had considered keeping some items of furniture in storage until such time that she moved to a house or apartment of her own. Now she wanted the equivalent of their value in either money or stocks. Before the day was over, even her lawyer occasionally glanced at her with something like admiration. She was driving a hard bargain.

That evening she returned to her hotel room, totally exhausted. Kicking off her shoes, she lay back on her bed.

"You don't know how glad I'll be to get all this over," she groaned wearily. "Did you sleep all day?" He looked fresh and relaxed.

"No, but I did snatch a couple of hours," he replied. He studied her tired features for a moment.

"Go ahead. What is it?" she encouraged him, sensing that he wanted to say something.

"What are you going to do about the alimony?" he asked abruptly.

Charlene raised herself up long enough to push the spare pillow over behind her back. It would be silly to pretend not to understand his question. All day she'd been mulling things over in her mind, trying to be fair to everyone—Paul and Burt and herself.

"I managed to find out today that Florida has a six months' residency requirement for divorce. My attorney's secretary looked it up for me. So it looks as though we won't be able to get married until next January, when the year of separation from Paul is up. It'll be just as fast to get the divorce in Georgia." She paused, gathering her courage. It had been such a damnably long day.

"There's the possibility I could go to some other state and get a divorce sooner than that, but I'd rather not. This way we can both have an opportunity to back out." She pushed herself up into a sitting position, uncomfortably aware of his rapierlike gaze trained unwaveringly upon her face. Suddenly she doubted herself. Maybe she should just gamble everything on the chance that Burt would marry her when the time came. If she refused alimony from Paul, perhaps she could raise herself a notch in Burt's opinion. But, no, she just couldn't dispense with her better judgement.

"If it will make you feel better, I won't touch a penny of the alimony money between now and January," she offered. "If we go ahead and get married when my divorce goes through, I'll give the money back to Paul."

As soon as she had finished, Burt was up and headed toward the door. She heard him mutter something under his breath that sounded like "poor bastard." Before she could ask him where he was going, the door had closed behind him. With a deep sigh of regret, she realized that obviously she had fallen even lower in his estimation. She closed her eyes and simultaneously her mind. Some time later the sound of the door opening awakened her. Burt was back.

At first she was on edge, expecting him to bring up the subject of the alimony and their marriage again, but when he didn't, she gradually relaxed. They went to dinner and then came back to the room. After ten years of marriage, she had little problem adjusting to the presence of a man in her hotel room, especially one she knew as well as Burt. Without any sense of embarrassment, she changed into her night-gown and settled comfortably in bed, thankful that he wasn't one of those nervous people who talked constantly and had to be doing something every minute. He didn't make her feel at all apologetic that she wasn't more entertaining. The last thing she remembered she was trying doggedly to keep her eyelids up during the evening news. They dropped like lead weights.

When she awoke the next morning, her head rested comfortably on only one pillow and she was snug under the light warmth of a blanket. Burt must have tucked her in last night, she reflected with bemusement, turning on her side and looking at him as he lay asleep in the other bed, the sheet drawn up just to his waist and his upper torso bare.

Suddenly his eyes opened and swung quickly around the room before finding her. She watched, intrigued, as his momentary confusion cleared, and he figured out where he was and why. It made him distinctly ill at ease to awaken and find her observing him in the defenseless state of sleep.

"Good morning," she said cheerfully, smiling.

As he swung his legs abruptly to the floor and sat on the edge of the bed, rubbing one hand roughly across his face, Charlene was forced to realize that he had slept naked. A stir of awareness took her completely by surprise. So absorbed had she been in the whole mystery of pregnancy, she had temporarily forgotten about sex, but the sight of Burt's nude body, sinewy and masculine and darkened by the Florida sun, awakened it with a resounding force. All he felt at the moment, though, was acute embarrassment over this waking intimacy.

"Sorry," he muttered, looking down at himself and hastily pulling the sheet across his loins to satisfy the minimal demands of propriety. "Never could sleep in pajamas."

In the effort to relieve his discomfort, Charlene unwillingly deprived herself of the sensual pleasure of looking at him. Turning over on her back again, she punched her pillow so that it elevated her head higher.

"I must have gone out like a light last night," she commented lightly.

"You did. Right in the middle of a pantyhose commercial," he confirmed, the tinge of humor in his voice reassuring her that he had collected his poise. Rolling her head sideways, she saw that his eyes were studying the swelling curve of her stomach beneath the covers. For the first time since she had become pregnant, she felt an unfamiliar stab of regret for the loss of her female allure. Quickly and resolutely she squashed the feeling. If she had to sacrifice sex for the thrill of feeling life moving inside her, it was well worth it. When her figure was returned to normal, Burt would want her again. Until then she would be patient and wait.

Chapter Seven

Charlene approached the matter of living quarters in Florida as tactfully as possible on the plane flight there.

"Don't you mind moving off your sailboat onto land?" she queried, remembering the steep companionway ladder and the compact interior of his boat. Comprehension glinted in the blue of his eyes as they met her hesitant brown ones.

"I already live on land. There was a house on the boatyard property when I bought it. If you're thinking about *Circe*, I sold her in March to a young fellow who plans to sail around the world."

Charlene was shocked, almost dismayed.

"But you seemed to love that boat! You had done so much work on it!" she protested.

He shrugged.

"A boat like that needs constant care, and I just don't have the time anymore—or the interest either. I get enough of boats working with them five and sometimes six days a week. I can always get another one if I want to, maybe something in fiberglass this time and easier to maintain."

She mulled over these words, thinking to herself how much there was about him she didn't know.

His house came as a delightful surprise. Made of stucco and painted a melon pink, it was located within walking distance of his boatyard on the southeastern coast of Florida, near the small town of Stewart. The fenced yard was a charming jungle of tropical foliage with hibiscus and bougainvillea. In the back yard were citrus trees.

Charlene sat on the patio the day after arriving, having awakened to find Burt already gone. Basking in the warm morning sunlight, she found it impossible to be discontented about anything, including the fact that Burt intended the two of them to sleep in separate bedrooms. He hadn't made any big production of it. He had just carried her luggage to what obviously had been a spare bedroom and said, "This is your room."

Her instinct was to protest the arrangement, but she decided to bide her time. It couldn't be easy for a man to make the adjustment from confirmed bachelor to living in the same house with a decidedly pregnant woman. She would have liked to mention the fact that sex wasn't taboo for her in her condition, but she simply did not have the nerve. He had eyed her figure that first day in her hotel room in

Atlanta and asked if she "minded." Since he carefully refrained from touching her at all, she could only guess that he would be repulsed by any sexual overtures she might make toward him.

For the time being she would abide by the "don't rock the boat" philosophy, adapting herself to his routine and changing his life as little as possible. It would be helpful to her if he would volunteer a little more information as to his likes and dislikes.

Today, for example, she didn't know if she should prepare lunch for the two of them. Since the boatyard wasn't far away, he could easily come home to eat. Quickly following that thought came the realization that there was little food in the refrigerator. She had checked it this morning when she fixed herself some breakfast. Until her car was delivered from Louisiana, she didn't even have a way to get to the supermarket to buy groceries. She was virtually stranded!

Undaunted by her situation, she busied herself around the house, acquainting herself with each room. Then at noon Burt arrived, a bag of hamburgers and French fries in his hand. Charlene noted that he wore denim work clothes and looked more like a regular working man than the owner of a shipyard.

"When will Ronnie be bringing my car?" she asked over lunch and then hastened to add that she would have gone to the grocery store that morning had she had some means of transportation. She didn't know what there was about the inquiry to make Burt look so odd.

"He has classes at college on the weekdays. He'll be driving your car here this weekend." His expression and tone were distant, as though his thoughts were elsewhere. Charlene wished now she hadn't mentioned the car. The atmosphere between them during lunch had been pleasantly relaxed.

"I see you have frozen steaks in the freezer. I can thaw those out for dinner," she suggested, not wanting to be too presumptuous and just take it upon herself to plan meals.

Crumpling up the paper that had been wrapped around his hamburger, Burt frowned.

"I don't expect you to cook for me, you know," he said abruptly.

Charlene's face revealed her amazement.

"What *do* you expect me to do?" she blurted curiously. "I have to do *something!*"

Regretfully, that comment hadn't gone across any better than the inquiry about the car. The cynical expression in his blue eyes said it hadn't taken her long to become bored, just one morning on her own in an entirely new environment.

"All I meant," she explained patiently, "is that I'm perfectly healthy. Except for horseback riding or something equally unwise, I can do most of the things I've always done. So don't expect me to turn into an invalid. The *only* reason I asked about the car was that I thought it would be easy for me to do things like grocery shopping while you're at work."

To her mild exasperation, she suspected she hadn't convinced him, and then that same afternoon she knew she hadn't when a rental car was delivered to her door. If she hadn't thought she might just make matters worse, she would have refused to sign for it.

During that first, awkward week, she had to keep reminding herself it hadn't always been easy when she and Paul were first married and getting used to living with each other. But living with Burt was nerve-wrackingly like picking her way through a mine field. Something as inconsequential as deciding what television program to watch became fraught with ridiculous tension.

"It doesn't matter to me," she would answer, not wanting to choose something that would bore him. "What would you rather watch?" But he was as noncommittal as she was. "Let's just watch whatever you *usually* watch," she would end up saying, hoping that he understood she was trying to be as little a disruptive force in his life as possible. But he was obviously not pleased, and they ended up watching something neither of them might have wished to watch, in awkward silence.

As much as Charlene wished her relationship with Burt could be more relaxed, she lived with the optimism that things would work out eventually. Nothing had the power to upset her for long. Somewhere inside her was a little wellspring of serenity that made her enjoy each little task she performed around the house, which seemed to her to sparkle under her care. It seemed to have its own cheerful personality.

Burt had made it plain from the outset that she had his permission to change the house in any way she desired. When time passed and she kept it just as it was, he brought up the subject again.

"But it's perfect just the way it is," she replied in all sincerity. If their relationship had been more open, she would have confided that the house suited her because it reflected his personality. In time, she would bring up the subject of a room for the baby, but that could wait until later.

Just when she would begin to tell herself that she was making headway toward understanding him, something else would happen to prove how little she knew of what went on in his head.

One day he came home for lunch earlier than was his habit and found her in the midst of cleaning the refrigerator. All of its contents were strewn around on the counters, causing the kitchen to look like more of a disaster area than it really was. Charlene was flustered and at the same time amused at her reaction. She was acting like a new bride found wanting in her housekeeping skills!

"You're early!" she said in a mockingly accusing voice.

He looked around at the chaos and then at her, making her self-consciously aware that she looked a mess. Her hair had gotten long and she had it tied back with a narrow red ribbon. As soon as she finished with the refrigerator, she had intended to change clothes and put on some makeup before he arrived home.

"Maybe you ought to hire a maid," he said unexpectedly.

"A maid!" Charlene couldn't contain her astonishment at the suggestion. "This house is too small to need a maid!" Then lest he take the comment as a criticism of the house, she continued in a joking tone, "Unless you're just finding fault with my housekeeping. This is not as bad as it looks, you know."

His expression didn't lighten.

"We don't have to live in this house," he said seriously. "You can look around for something larger . . ."

"Don't be silly!" Charlene broke in, genuinely exasperated at him for putting such an interpretation upon her words. "I don't want to move into another house. I like this one fine! All I meant was that I'm perfectly capable of taking care of this one myself—without the help of a maid."

To emphasize her point, she turned back to the refrigerator and began to fill it up again. When the kitchen was restored to perfect order, she set the table with new cloth placemats and matching napkins. For lunch she had made a shrimp salad, which looked tempting served on beds of crisp lettuce.

"Isn't this elegant?" she commented with whimsical lightness as they sat down to eat. "I should have bought a bottle of white wine."

When he said nothing at all during the entire meal, she wondered if he were still dwelling on their earlier exchange about a maid and moving to a larger house. Finally, she could stand the silence no longer.

"Is anything wrong?" she asked.

"You don't have to go to all this trouble to make lunch for me," he said hesitantly, gesturing at the table with its crisp placemats and cloth napkins. Then at the sight of the disappointment clouding her face, he grimaced. "Don't get me wrong," he added quickly. "I appreciate all your efforts. It's just that I want you to feel free to go out to lunch with other people whenever you want to. I can always fix myself a sandwich or pick up a hamburger. It's what I've done for years."

As much as she might appreciate his not wanting her to feel tied down to a domestic schedule, she was deeply disappointed that he obviously didn't know she looked forward to his coming home for lunch each day. She took pleasure in preparing a variety of light meals they both would enjoy. It hurt her feelings to be told outright that he would just as soon make himself a sandwich and eat it alone.

"I don't know anybody to go out to lunch with yet," she said when she was able to produce a voice carefully free of emotion. "But when I do, I'll keep that in mind."

After he had gone, she relived the exchange and saw it in a different light. Burt might be feeling locked in, knowing that she was home waiting for him each day to come for lunch. She waited a couple of days, not wanting to be too obvious, and made it a point to be away from the house at noon, leaving him a note on the kitchen table that she had gone shopping. She ate lunch alone at a little restaurant and wondered if he missed her at all or if he were relieved to have the time alone. *You've got to be patient,* she told herself, munching without enthusiasm on her spinach quiche.

When a whole month had passed and Burt hadn't made an offer to show her his boatyard, she began to wonder if he were ashamed to have people see her. Or was his work an area of his life he didn't want her intruding into? One evening she approached the matter obliquely when the opportunity presented itself in a most unlikely way.

They were sitting in the living room watching the news before dinner. The baby was even more active than usual and dealt her a kick under the ribs that made her grunt aloud. She looked over to find Burt looking at her with mixed curiosity and concern.

"It's got to be a boy," she said, grinning. Suddenly she wanted more than anything to share with Burt the way it felt to have this squirming, kicking life inside her. "Would you like to feel it move?" she asked diffidently.

He stared back as though he weren't sure he had heard her right. Her disappointment at his reaction was too crushing to hide, even if she had wanted to. He had insisted upon his rights and responsibilities as the father. The least he could do was show a little interest!

For a long moment his eyes probed the hurt rebelliousness in hers and then surprisingly he got up from his chair and came over to sit beside her on the sofa. She held her breath while his hand came over and rested on the tight drum of her stomach. They waited together for several seconds and then the baby kicked again. Charlene's eyes held his for a strangely charged moment.

"Doesn't that feel strange?" he murmured, fascinated and perhaps a little repelled, too, at the notion of having one's body invaded by another life.

"*Very* strange, at first," she agreed, secretly pleased that he left his hand there. She would have liked to question him about his feelings. How did *he* feel knowing he was half responsible for that life moving under his hand? The question she asked instead was proof of how closed were the channels of communication between them.

"Burt . . . do the people who work for you at the boatyard know about me?"

He took his hand away and looked at her in surprise.

"Why, sure, they do. Why do you ask?"

"They know I'm living here in this house and pregnant with your baby?" she persisted.

"Sure," he said again, regarding her with a puzzled frown, failing to follow this line of questioning.

"Would it be embarrassing to you if I came over to boatyard one day and saw it?"

"Hell, no," he denied without any hesitation, but was obviously taken aback at the question. Comprehending her thinking now, his expression turned vaguely apologetic. "It just never occurred to me you'd be interested," he said with simple honesty.

It was opportune that the baby delivered another vigorous kick. Charlene winced and got up to go and check on the roast. At times like this one, she despaired of ever understanding Burt. How could he want to marry her, take care of her and their child, if he thought she wouldn't even be interested in seeing the business where he spent most of his waking time?

The next afternoon she took nerve in hand and walked the short distance to the boatyard. The longer she stayed away, the more difficult it would be for her to enter his working world, and she was determined not to be relegated to the role of outsider.

"Can I help you, ma'am?"

This curious inquiry came from a bearded young man who hurried up to her soon after she had wandered through the entrance. He wore paint-spattered blue overalls and stood a little impatiently and waited for her reply as she stared around her in fascination at a wide range of activity. She had never seen sailboats out of the water before and was amazed to see how *much* of them there was below the waterline.

The combined volume of noise came from all kinds of power tools wielded by a host of workers who, for the most part, were young like the bearded fellow awaiting an answer to his question. Now and then there would be a slight lull in the din and she could hear a radio playing rock music.

"Er . . . I'm looking for Burt," she said, her nerve failing her when it came right down to identifying herself.

"He's in the office. This way," he said politely, leading the way.

They entered a large metal building teeming with

activity like the yard outside. The main part of it was outfitted as a workshop with various types of saws and other machines whose purposes she couldn't guess. Through open doors she glimpsed storage rooms with shelves of inventory.

Burt was talking on the telephone and looked up when she stood uncertainly in the doorway of his office, having been abandoned by her guide and left to introduce herself. She motioned for Burt to go ahead with his phone call and walked a few steps into the office, pretending to look around, but actually trying to dispel the awkwardness she felt at being here. The intent blue gaze riveted upon her form did nothing to put her at ease.

"I decided to pay you a visit," she said unnecessarily when he hung up the phone. "It sure is busy around here."

He stood, but before he could speak, the telephone was ringing again. As he answered it, she could see in his expression the conflict being waged inside him. He was torn by conflicting demands, business and personal.

When he had concluded that conversation, she spoke hurriedly to put him at ease.

"I can see this isn't a good time for you to show me around. Don't worry about me. I just wanted to take a walk."

"My secretary is out on vacation this week," he said, giving a rueful glance around the office. "I should be in at least three other places right now, but I'm waiting for a couple of important calls, and I can't spare anybody out of the yard."

"Why don't I stay here this afternoon and answer the phone?" Charlene offered impulsively. "I don't have anything else to do. If you have time, you could show me around later."

Instinctively he was about to refuse her offer and then checked himself.

"Are you sure you wouldn't mind?"

"Positive," she declared. "Maybe I can help out with something else while I'm sitting here."

"You'll be helping out more than enough if you just answer the phone," he assured her and then left.

As it turned out, she was kept fairly busy for the next couple of hours. When Burt came back at about four-thirty, he was wearing a pair of overalls like those the yard crew wore. She recited the list of callers and relayed the messages she had written down.

"We're about to put a boat back in the water," he said when she had finished. "Want to come and watch?"

Her face lit with enthusiasm. Maybe he wasn't keeping her sequestered here in the office out of sight after all!

"I'd love to," she said eagerly, getting up from behind the desk.

"Don't be surprised if somebody calls you Mrs. Burt," he said with studied casualness. "The guys here at the yard think we're already married."

Charlene worked at accustoming herself to that revelation as she accompanied Burt outside and watched as a sleek sailboat was transferred by the big travel lift from its place on shore, where big power jacks had kept it propped up, to the water. Sensing something of the drama of the moment, she held her breath from time to time, releasing it in relief when the boat floated safely in the water.

When applause rose from the crew of workers, she wondered if there had indeed been an element of suspense—perhaps even danger—in the procedure she had just watched. It had all looked faultlessly smooth and professional to her. She looked questioningly at Burt, who was approaching her now.

"Okay, wise guys, I know the rules!" he yelled good-naturedly, grinning. "Before you head for the nearest bar, come over here and meet my wife."

Afterwards he explained that whenever he kept his boatyard employees past the usual closing time, as he had done this afternoon, the drinks were on him at a local bar where most of them stopped off on their way home.

"I'll bet you used to go there, too," Charlene said with immediate insight.

The movement of his shoulders acknowledged the accuracy of her guess. "Sometimes I did. There wasn't any reason to be in a hurry to go home."

Spoken with no irony to rob it of sincerity, the comment warmed Charlene's insides. She couldn't have been more pleased if he had come home with a dozen long-stemmed roses. It was the first clue she had that Burt might find some pleasure in her presence in his house and life.

After that day she felt free to go to the boatyard any time she wanted to, and she went there nearly every day, at first using the excuse that the distance was perfect for a walk and she needed exercise. Before long, she was greeted by the yard workers as a familiar figure. When she showed a willingness to help out in the office whenever needed or to run errands in her car, she became accepted as a part of the working operation.

Burt's secretary, Cindy, turned out to be a fresh, pretty girl in her twenties with long, silky blond hair and a figure that bordered on voluptuous. Charlene liked her upon first sight and derided herself for secret pangs of jealousy. She did her best not to think of Burt spending hours at work in the proximity of such female comeliness and then coming home to her with her burgeoning figure.

His growing solicitude made her feel protected and secure, but she wished at times he would show some awareness of *her* as a woman, a person apart from the child she carried. All his concern seemed prompted by consideration for their unborn baby's well-being. The constraint that had initially held him back from touching her diminished, it seemed to her, in direct proportion to her increase in ungainliness. She reveled in the touch of his hands, their strength and gentleness, as he performed numerous thoughtful little services: helping her into the car, propelling her firmly toward a chair and taking over whatever task she insisted she was still perfectly capable of doing, even removing her shoes and massaging her feet.

Sometimes she wondered what his attitude would

be toward her when she and the baby were no longer a single, grotesque body. Would he touch her so frequently like this when she was back to normal? Such introspection stirred unease, and she pushed it away, allowing nothing to blight her spirits for long.

Finally the time came when she was actually awaiting the trip to the hospital. Her suitcase was packed in readiness, and Burt seemed to be calling from the boatyard or dropping by the house every five minutes. Charlene felt as if she had been pregnant forever. It was difficult to remember now what it had felt like *not* having this squirming, urgent life inside her. She was ready to hold her baby in her arms, eager to see him or her as a tiny individual.

Several times she had raised the question of a room for the baby, but Burt had evaded it each time. For a while the bassinet placed in a corner of her own room would be an adequate arrangement. She was hoping things would take a normal course after she had recovered from the delivery, and she and Burt would start sleeping in the same room together like a normal husband and wife, even though they weren't really husband and wife at all yet. But she felt like Mrs. Burt Landry because everybody called her that. She even signed her name like that on checks written on her joint checking account with Burt.

In January she would be free to marry Burt in reality, if he still wanted to marry her. She was sure that she wanted to marry him. It was quite beyond her capabilities to envision life without Burt Landry.

What ironies life could hold for a person! she mused. In the ignorance of youth, she had passed up Burt and then had the good luck to have another chance to appreciate his fineness. She was a lucky woman.

A lucky woman . . .

She kept hearing that phrase during the week she spent in the hospital following her delivery of a seven-pound boy. "You're a lucky woman, Mrs. Landry," the doctor and the nurses told her, "to have a normal delivery after all." The motherly nurse's aides who brought her baby to her at intervals throughout the day and night extolled her luck at having such a handsome, healthy boy. Charlene agreed with all of them, but privately she counted high among her blessings her luck in having Burt, the father of her child. How could she ever have thought she wanted to go through this whole experience of having a baby alone?

She looked forward eagerly to his visits. His face had been tense with anxiety that first day. He had come up close to the bed and taken her proffered hand, gripping it tightly while his eyes searched her face and then stared down at the strange new flatness of her stomach. She had kept reassuring him she really was fine.

"Have you seen the baby?" she had asked.

"Not yet," he answered distractedly.

Charlene had felt guilty at being so pleased. What kind of mother was she to be glad Burt had come to see her first?

At her urging, Burt perched carefully on the edge

of her bed, while she introduced the subject of a name for their child.

"We never really did decide," she reminded him. "What about Edward after your father and Theodore after Cappy? We can call him Ted."

"Edward Theodore," he repeated, raising his eyebrows skeptically, but looking pleased nonetheless. "That's a lot of name for a little kid."

Watching the play of emotion on his face aroused a powerful surge of tenderness inside Charlene. She wanted to say or do something demonstrative to express the way she felt, but he already felt shy and awkward with his present situation.

"I'll walk down to the nursery with you," she offered, suddenly eager for him to see their baby.

He drew back in surprise.

"You mean you can already walk?" he inquired skeptically.

"The more I move around, the faster I'll recover," she assured him, getting carefully out of the bed and letting him help her into the robe lying at the foot. They walked slowly down the hospital corridor, her arm linked in his.

In front of the nursery window, Charlene couldn't resist a surreptitious glance at Burt's face as he stared through the plate glass at the tiny, red-faced sleeping infant, one minuscule hand clutching his cheek. Perhaps Burt was trying to make the mental adjustment between her swollen stomach with its kicking movements and that perfectly formed little human being beyond the glass of the nursery. Perhaps he was thinking what most people did—that he was in the presence of a miracle. But his only comment was "He sure is little."

"Edward Theodore does seem like quite a label for one that size," Charlene commented drolly.

On the way back to her room, she announced that she would be able to go home on Friday.

"That soon?" was his immediate and disappointing response. He seemed even more distracted and almost nervous during the remainder of his visit. She reminded herself that he was probably uneasy at the prospect of having a newborn infant in the house, but when presented with the reality, she was confident he would quickly adjust.

Every day after that he came to visit, and each time Charlene felt stronger and more like her old self. It was going to be great *not* to be pregnant!

"I can't wait to get back home," she would say and then have to try to hide her disappointment that he showed so little enthusiasm over the prospect himself. There would be a swift flash of something like apprehension in his blue eyes. She worried that these days of her absence from his house would have rekindled old memories of what it was to live in solitude. Did he dread having his privacy invaded again? Charlene lay awake through much of that last night in the hospital, pondering these disturbing questions.

Chapter Eight

*I*n her excitement over going home, she didn't notice at first that he was going the wrong way. When she finally saw that he couldn't possibly be taking her straight home, she asked, "Where are you going?"

His reply was cryptic.

"I want to show you something."

Charlene bit back the impulse to protest that today was hardly a time when she felt up to sight-seeing. She wanted to get Ted home and settled into his new environment. Now that she thought about it, Burt had been acting strangely ever since he arrived at the hospital to pick them up. He was never extremely talkative, but today he had hardly said a word, even in response to her direct questions.

Apprehension built inside her as they drove along in utter silence.

When he turned into the pillared and landscaped entrance of Atlantic Heights, one of the most exclusive country club developments in the county, Charlene was totally nonplussed. Why was Burt taking them in here? They didn't even have any friends in Atlantic Heights.

An ominous suspicion formed in her mind like a faint dark cloud and grew rapidly larger and blacker as he drove with some apparent destination along the streets lined with large, handsome homes. With a deft turn of the wheel, he pulled into the driveway of a rambling, Spanish-style house with a red-tiled roof and lacy wrought-iron grillwork. A realtor's FOR SALE sign had SOLD diagonally across the middle of it.

Charlene stared at the house and the sign and then over at Burt with wide-eyed consternation. Surely he *hadn't* . . . he *wouldn't* . . . Her mind fumbled desperately in search of some reassurance that what she was beginning to suspect wasn't really true.

"You don't like it," he said bleakly, frowning at her reaction.

"I do!" she said hastily, summoning all those faculties for polite deception that had grown rusty with disuse over the past months when she had found little need for a social manner. "I like it *very* much! It's a beautiful house—and the landscaping is perfect! Have you—I mean, *are* you—?" She struggled helplessly to ask the question whose answer was looking more affirmative every second. Burt was digging in his trouser pocket and producing a key.

"I hope you really *do* like it," he said grimly. "Because it's yours."

"Let's take Ted inside and look at it, then," she murmured. "This is such a . . . surprise."

Waves of sick disappointment were spreading through her, making it impossible to act enthusiastic. She had so looked forward to coming home to the bright, homey, little pink stucco house. Burt hadn't said "it's *ours*." He had said "it's *yours*." Did that mean he didn't intend to live with them in this enormous house? If that turned out to be the case, she would put up a fight.

She was somewhat reassured when she saw that he had moved all the furniture from the smaller house into this one. Evidently he *did* plan to live here, too. Her heart squeezed painfully at the sight of the familiar furnishings, virtually lost and looking somehow sad over their inadequacy to fill these much larger rooms. And indeed some of the rooms had no furniture at all.

The house was comparable to the one she and Paul had owned in Atlanta and sold in July following their separation. The carpet and wallpaper and paneling were all professionally coordinated. Charlene exclaimed over the size and design of the kitchen with its many gadgets and solid oak cabinets, but underneath the praise was a bleak hollowness. She had been more than happy with the little kitchen in the other house.

The only truly bright spot in the tour of the house

was the nursery. Burt had gone out, ostensibly on his own, and bought baby furniture. In addition to the crib and chest of drawers were units of wall shelves arranged with colorful stuffed animals and brightly painted toys. The sight of this room brought tears to Charlene's eyes.

"I love it!" she said with difficulty.

"I know the house looks pretty bare," Burt apologized as she laid Ted in his bassinet in the bedroom that contained her same furniture from the other house. "I didn't want to buy furniture myself. You're much better qualified to do that than I am. I want you to replace all this old stuff—and don't worry about the cost, either. Get whatever you want."

Charlene was leaning over the bassinet. She stayed there longer than necessary, fussing with Ted as if she were trying to make him more comfortable. When she straightened up, she had managed to quell the ache of disappointment that threatened to erupt into tears. At all costs she wanted to spare Burt's feelings. He had bought this house for the three of them to live in. She was just going to have to make the best of it, but right now she was overwhelmingly tired.

"I hope you don't mind," she said, mustering a weary smile, "but I think I'd like to lie down and rest a little while."

He was instantly contrite.

"I hope this wasn't too much for you," he said in a concerned voice. "You just get into bed. If you need something, let me know."

Charlene got into her nightgown and lay down in her familiar bed, letting the tears slide out now and roll wetly down her cheeks. Under different circumstances she could have been happy with Burt's "surprise," but it only emphasized the lack of any real communication between them. He had kept suggesting she change the little stucco house, and she had repeatedly told him she loved it just as it was. Evidently he had not believed her. Perhaps he had put his own interpretation upon her lack of interest in redecorating it. He might have thought she considered it unworthy of her attention, or not having enough potential for her to bother with it.

That first day they had run into each other in the marina last February, she had told him about her life with Paul, how she spent much of her time and energy decorating new houses and entertaining. But she had been another person then. Now, she had new interests, a whole different scale of values. The prospect of furnishing and decorating yet another large house held no appeal for her unless Burt wanted the house for himself, too, not just for her.

After some minutes of this dreary introspection, she felt herself growing drowsy and welcomed the respite of sleep. She was probably just tired. Everything would appear in a more cheerful light after she had rested.

Some time later she was awakened by lusty wailing from the bassinet. If Ted had gone through a preliminary stage of fussing, she hadn't heard him. No doubt she would become more finely attuned to his needs as time went by.

187

Getting out of bed, she picked him up and made soothing sounds as she sat on the edge of the bed and nursed him. After a week she still wasn't entirely accustomed to either the sight or the feel of that hungry little mouth sucking at her breast. Some sixth sense rather than an actual sound told her they were being watched. She looked around and saw Burt standing in the open doorway.

"Come join us," she invited with a smile. After the nap she felt refreshed and more optimistic in general. It was important to her that Burt not feel excluded from her relationship with the baby.

He came into the room and at her urging, sat on the edge of the bed next to her, watching the nursing procedure with absorbed interest.

"You decided to nurse him after all," he said after a silence during which they both listened to the loud sucking and swallowing sounds. "You said you weren't sure you would."

"I wasn't sure at first if I was going to like it," she explained. "For one thing, it hurt more than I had expected, but now I'm beginning to get used to it. And everything I read on the subject said mother's milk is much better for a baby than any formula. The baby gets all kinds of immunities from the mother's body and—" Suddenly she broke off with a laugh, wrinkling her nose in a wry expression. "You must find this fascinating conversation," she joked lightly.

But Burt's expression was still thoughtfully serious.

"But you'll be the only one who can feed him," he

pointed out after a moment. "Isn't that going to tie you down?"

Charlene was taken aback.

"I plan to take care of him myself!" she exclaimed. "I have no intention of leaving him with anyone else!" Then she added in a moderating tone, "He *can* take a bottle with formula, too, in addition to nursing."

It puzzled her that this last information was a source of satisfaction to Burt, but before long she understood the reason.

"I didn't get a chance to tell you earlier, but I paid the membership fee to join the Atlantic Heights Country Club. There's an eighteen-hole golf course and a dozen tennis courts and two Olympic-sized swimming pools," he announced casually.

Charlene felt the light bulb of understanding flash brilliantly over her head. Now she knew why Burt was worried that she might tie herself down nursing the baby. Not only had he purchased this big, expensive house, which she was to decorate and furnish, but he had joined the country club so that she could become involved once again in playing tennis. For the second time today, he was presenting her with a *fait accompli* she must pretend to like or else risk hurting his feelings.

"It will be a while before Ted here can join the club swim team!" she quipped, hoping to pass the subject off lightly for the time being. She had no intention of getting involved again in country club activities, not right now while Ted was a baby.

Maybe Burt could get a refund on his membership money.

"I'm going to have my hands full taking care of him and this big house," she added, not seeing the danger until it was too late.

"You'll need a maid," Burt said immediately, the thought obviously not a new one.

Charlene was swept by the strange, panicky sensation that she was being ushered along a corridor against her will by someone with the best intentions. She didn't *want* this big house with or without a maid, nor did she want to join into the world of country club life again. She had enjoyed it once, but right now she preferred to do other things. The problem was convincing Burt without hurting his feelings.

It occurred to her suddenly that perhaps she was misconstruing the whole situation by jumping to the conclusion that the house and the club membership were solely for *her*. Perhaps Burt wanted them for himself, too. After all, he was a successful man in terms of income. He could afford a country club style of living if he desired it. Charlene decided just to hold her tongue for a while and see for herself if he showed signs of wanting a more luxurious home environment.

Ted had fallen asleep in the midst of nursing. Burt reached over and very gently picked up one of the tiny, perfect hands that clutched instinctively around a large, tanned finger.

"Would you like to hold him?" Charlene offered

impulsively, expecting him to refuse. Men were almost without exception frightened of handling newborn infants.

"I wouldn't want to hurt him," Burt said uncertainly, reluctant and yet obviously wanting to take her up on the offer.

Charlene had to hide her surprise.

"You won't hurt him," she said matter-of-factly, lifting the sleeping baby with both hands and handing him to Burt. "He's like a little bundle of rags. You just have to support his head."

As if to demonstrate her confidence in his ability, she got up and went into the bathroom. When she returned, Burt was in the process of laying the baby in the bassinet.

"You already look like an old expert at that," she commented in all seriousness. There wasn't any reason she should be surprised. She knew the gentleness and adeptness of those hands herself. It was hard not to envy her diminutive son their attention.

Before the weekend was over, it was clear to Charlene that Burt was going to be one of those fathers, rare in her own experience, who was both willing and eager to do his fair share in tending his child. He balked at nothing, including changing diapers. After that initial awkwardness, he handled the baby with as much skill as Charlene did herself.

He seemed intrigued with his tiny offspring, an interest that showed no sign of lessening in the weeks that followed. The greater distance from the house to the boatyard made it impractical for him to come home for lunch, but in the afternoon when he returned from work, he went directly to his son's bassinet, or if Charlene happened to be holding the baby, he would take him away from her at the first opportunity. On weekends he urged her to go shopping or do whatever she might like to do on her own while he babysat. He reminded her that she had said the baby could take a bottle in her absence.

"Why are you always trying to get rid of me!" Charlene protested sometimes, laughing. Underneath, her feelings were really smarting with hurt. At the risk of sounding jealous, she wished Burt would show just a particle of that interest in *her!*

With Christmas only a few weeks away, she began to take advantage of getting away from the house and doing some shopping on her own. If they were going to live in the house permanently, she had to begin furnishing it. Burt kept asking her when she was going to buy new furniture, and it was time she transformed the house into a real home.

One room that figured largely into her plans was the big, completely empty room that obviously was intended to be the master bedroom. But first, she would give her attention to the den and the breakfast room adjoining the kitchen. By then, she might have worked up her nerve. The formal living and dining rooms could wait.

Christmas was only a week away when the den furniture was delivered. That same afternoon Charlene was toweling off following a shower when Burt arrived home from work. She had had a busy day, wanting the den to be perfect when he saw it, right down to a beautifully shaped Christmas tree waiting to be decorated.

"Charly?" She heard him call out as he entered the house from the garage. Her heart began to pump harder as she realized he would be standing there in the door of her bedroom in just a few seconds. Six-week-old Ted still slept in the bassinet, which she had not moved from her bedroom, the ostensible reason being that she could tend to him easily during the night. Of equal importance was the fact that its presence meant Burt entered her room at will, and he hadn't before.

"In here, Burt!" she called, dropping the towel to the floor with a deliberate motion and opening a bureau drawer containing her underwear. She was lifting out a pair of panties, having taken her time, when he walked through the open door with no warning of what he would see. He stopped in mid-stride, shock in his blue eyes as they ran quickly over her.

"Hi. Welcome home," she greeted with a smile, trying to sound as though it were altogether ordinary for him to see her naked. At least he didn't look as though the sight of her body repulsed him. She was conscious of his intent gaze the whole time she stepped into her panties and drew them up and then slipped her arms into her bra and settled it over her breasts, which were still larger than their normal size before her pregnancy.

"The den furniture came today," she said conversationally, walking over to her closet and taking a pair of slacks off the hanger. They fit as well now as they had before she became pregnant. "I hope you like it," she continued, stepping into the slacks and pulling them up. "Guess what else I bought?" she inquired gaily, turning back to the closet for her blouse.

"What did you buy?" he asked mechanically, speaking for the first time.

"A Christmas tree!" she answered, knowing even before she looked around that he wasn't watching her anymore. As she buttoned up her blouse and tucked it into her slacks, she observed Burt as he leaned over the bassinet, a smile on his lips as the chubby baby awakened with a huge yawn. His arms and legs churned excitedly at the sight of his father and the sound of his voice as Burt inquired in a more normal-sounding voice, "Been a good fellow today?"

By now Charlene was used to this close rapport between father and son and found it charming, but her attention this afternoon was drawn to the way Burt's shirt stretched across his shoulders and back, emphasizing the taut body underneath. Her hands tingled at the memory of how it had felt to stroke those firm contours. She longed now for the freedom to walk up beside him at the bassinet and slide her hand across the warm, vibrant flesh underneath the plain work shirt.

She watched, feeling totally excluded and ignored, as Burt picked up the baby and carried him on his shoulder toward the threshold of her room.

"Coming?" he inquired, turning around and looking back at her.

She managed the semblance of a smile as her dark eyes met the wary blue of his.

"In just a minute," she said tonelessly.

It was getting more and more difficult for her to act as though everything were just fine between them, when as far as she was concerned, things were terribly wrong. Why didn't Burt want to make love to her now? Did a woman lose her sex appeal just because she had borne a child?

Sighing her despondency, she picked up the damp towel from the floor and carried it back into the bathroom. Maybe she should call the furniture store and cancel that bedroom furniture. What if the whole thing backfired in her face and Burt refused to sleep with her in that king-sized bed?

If only she could fathom what went on in that head of his. He had to know on the basis of their affair last February and March that she had all the sensual needs of a normal woman. Did he no longer desire her? Did he expect her to abstain indefinitely from sex? How was he satisfying *his* needs?

This last question always brought a sharp stir of emotion she recognized as jealousy. Just the mental vision of Cindy, his sexy young secretary, aroused a savage kind of possessiveness she hadn't ever known before now. It was strange to her that she hadn't suffered this much anguish over Paul even when she knew for certain he was being unfaithful to her.

Burt's pleasure over the den made her forget her frustration for the time being.

"You weren't kidding when you said you know your decorating," he commented with open admiration when she walked into the den a few minutes later. "It looks great in here. The couch and chairs are comfortable, too. I tried them all out."

She felt herself glowing under the warmth of his approval and found it necessary to crack a joke.

"Maybe you'd better wait until you see the bill."

Actually she was only half-joking, since she didn't know if he did realize how expensive good furniture like this was. He had repeatedly given her *carte blanche* in furnishing the house.

"I'm not worried about the bill. Buy whatever you want. I can afford it," he said, not smiling with her. The set of his jaw and the tinge of grimness invited no further discussion of the subject.

Charlene wondered how many wives spent as much money as she had on this room and their husbands didn't even ask the amount. Here was just another example of how far they were from having a normal relationship.

"Have you met anybody who lives around here?" he asked her later over dinner. It wasn't the first time by far that he had made that inquiry, but tonight Charlene could give him an affirmative answer.

"The delivery van from the furniture store blocked the street for a few minutes today while the driver was trying to back into our driveway. I was standing outside with Ted, watching, and two women got out of their cars and came up on the lawn and introduced themselves.

"They were on their way to the tennis courts and

asked me if I play. I told them I used to. They invited me to come out on any Wednesday morning when all the courts are reserved for Women's Day."

Charlene's tone indicated her lack of interest in following up on the invitation, but Burt had stopped eating while she related the little incident.

"Why don't you go next Wednesday," he suggested promptly. "You should be able to meet some other players on your own level and then you could set up your own matches."

"I probably could," she admitted, "but I really don't have much interest right now in getting back into tennis."

But he wasn't content to drop the subject.

"You need to get out more and make friends. After you get the house furnished, you could invite people here for lunch. How's the new maid working out, by the way?"

At his insistence, she had finally hired a young Spanish woman to come in once a week to help with the cleaning.

"She's a big help," Charlene said absently, her mind absorbed with what he had said before the inquiry about the maid. This was as good a time as any to get something straight.

"If I'm going to invite people in the neighborhood over, I'd rather invite couples," she pointed out. "For dinner or cocktails or whatever—when *you're* here."

His expression repudiated the suggestion even before he said the first word.

"I'm sure I'd have a lot in common with these guys

around here. I see them driving home in their company Cadillacs and Mercedes, wearing suits and ties." His voice was edged with contempt and then became ironic as he continued. "Here I drive up—" He stopped abruptly, apparently hit by a sudden and not pleasant thought. His blue eyes were sharply questioning as they probed her puzzled brown ones. "Charly, does it embarrass you for the neighbors to see your husband—or at least the guy they *think* is your husband," he amended, "driving up in a pickup truck, wearing work clothes?"

Charlene produced a reply with some effort. He had just hit upon an extremely sensitive subject, but not the one she was primarily concerned about.

"Of course, it doesn't bother me," she scoffed. "What do I care what these people think?"

What she *did* care about was whether he still intended to marry her a month from now when her year's separation from Paul would be up and she would be eligible for divorce. There hadn't been any mention of their actually getting married since Atlanta. He had said he wanted his child to bear his name, but Ted's birth certificate already read Edward Theodore Landry. For all the fuss society made over marriage, virtually no one, it seemed, required actual proof of it. She had been admitted into the hospital as Mrs. Burt Landry, and nobody in Florida except Burt and herself knew anything different. Had he decided to forego the legal ceremony now that the myth had been established? That was hardly fair to her, but so far she hadn't mustered the nerve to confront him outright. In a way, it was better *not* knowing if he *didn't* intend to marry her.

The telephone rang just as she got up and began clearing the table.

"Please, would you get that?" she asked Burt, who had also gotten up and was helping her. In her present mood, she didn't want to talk to anyone, not even someone who had dialed a wrong number.

"Hi, Cindy, what's up?" he said when he had done her bidding and walked over to answer the wall phone.

Mention of his young secretary's name created a furor of jealousy inside Charlene. It didn't matter that, from what she could hear of the conversation on Burt's end, it concerned business, something to do about a lost invoice Cindy had located that afternoon after he had left the boatyard. Why couldn't she have waited until tomorrow to tell him? Was she trying to impress Burt with her diligence or was this all simply subterfuge? Were Burt and Cindy having an affair?

Charlene despised herself for harboring all these totally unfounded suspicions. She was acting like the soap-opera stereotype of a jealous wife. The worst part of it was that she had no real right to get up in arms over any relationship Burt had with another woman. Charlene *wasn't* his wife. Pretty soon she wouldn't be anybody's wife.

After he had hung up the phone, Burt came back to the table to help her finish clearing it. He never just got up and walked away after a meal, a habit she attributed to his having lived on his own and taken care of himself for so long. Tonight she found it heartbreakingly difficult to work side by side with him and yet not be free to touch him in the most casual way. How could she carry on a conversation with him when all these unanswered questions rang in her head? If she didn't watch herself, she would be asking him point-blank if there were now—or ever had been—anything between Cindy and him beside a working relationship.

"I'll finish up here," she suggested in a strained voice. "Why don't you check on the baby?"

She could feel his gaze on her back as she bent to place dishes in the dishwasher, but he didn't say anything, and a moment later he had gone, carrying out her request.

That night as she lay alone in her bed in the darkness, her depression culminated in a decision to cancel the order for the bedroom furniture first thing in the morning. Her situation seemed hopeless to her. But when she called the store the next day, she heard herself reconfirming the delivery date. "The day before Christmas Eve," she reiterated to the store manager. The meek might inherit the earth, but who was asking for the earth? Her expectations had always been reasonable her whole life, as they were now. All she asked was that Burt make love to her, sleep with her in the same bedroom, and marry her when she was legally free. Then she would be satisfied.

Chapter Nine

*E*verything possible went wrong . . .

The delivery truck didn't arrive on time. Charlene was wringing her hands and just on the verge of telephoning the manager to tell him he'd have to wait until tomorrow to bring the furniture when the truck driver called and said he would be there in fifteen minutes. He explained that he had been involved in a minor traffic accident that had delayed him. No one had been hurt and luckily her furniture wasn't damaged.

"I'm redecorating our bedroom as a surprise Christmas gift!" she said in exasperation. "It won't come as much of a surprise if my husband comes home while you're carrying the furniture into the house!"

The driver mentioned hesitantly that after today

there wouldn't be any more deliveries until after Christmas. The store employees didn't have to work on Christmas Eve.

Charlene was more than halfway sure that if she raised the roof, figuratively speaking, she *could* have the furniture delivered tomorrow, but after a pause she told the delivery man to come on if he could indeed be there in fifteen minutes. She would be cutting it closer than she liked, but there was still time to have the furniture arranged in the master bedroom and the finishing touches made to set the stage for tonight.

It turned out to be thirty minutes before the truck arrived. By the time it was pulling out of the driveway and leaving, she judged she had less than an hour before Burt would be home. If she hadn't decided to vacuum the carpet before she made up the bed, she would have known fate had betrayed her again. The noise of the vacuum cleaner motor kept her from hearing Burt call her name as he usually did when he walked into the house. But this time he was earlier than his usual time.

Several days earlier she had bought sheets and a matching spread for the new king-sized bed and washed and pressed the sheets. As she shook open the fitted sheet today, she thought again that it looked small. To her utter dismay, when she tried to put it on the mattress, she found that it didn't come close to stretching to fit all the corners. Evidently, an error had been made in packaging.

"Damn. *Damn! DAMN!*" she swore, getting successively louder as waves of frustration rolled over her. It was the last straw when she looked up and saw Burt standing in the open door with Ted in his arms.

"I didn't know you were home *already!*" she wailed miserably, wishing with all her heart the floor under her feet would open up and she could sink down out of sight, right down into the ground.

"I got here a few minutes ago," he said slowly, glancing around the bedroom at the new furniture and then bringing his gaze back to her where she sat slumped on the edge of the enormous, unmade bed. "I called out, but you didn't answer."

"The vacuum cleaner," she said in a low, abject voice, too mortified now to look at him. This had to rank as the worst moment of her life. His voice came hesitantly to her from where he stood in the doorway.

"You didn't mention you were buying furniture for this room."

Charlene summoned all her nerve and lifted her head to meet his eyes. They showed that he was aware of her discomfort and was not quite sure of how to proceed.

"It was going to be a surprise." Irritation returned as she thought of how everything had backfired. "But then the delivery truck was late . . . and the fitted sheet didn't *fit*—and you came home early." She balled up the offending sheet and threw it on the carpet to vent her helpless disgust.

"I could always leave and come back," he ventured, with seeming seriousness.

She looked questioningly at him for a moment and

saw the suppressed laughter illuminating his eyes. Her own lips quirked as she grudgingly acknowledged the humor in the situation. She must look and sound funny.

"I suppose it isn't the end of the world," she admitted sheepishly, enormously relieved that he seemed to put no special significance upon her secret furnishing of this particular room. Surely he must know it was the master bedroom.

She stood up and bent over to pick up the sheet she had hurled to the floor and began folding it.

"I can exchange this tomorrow. Most of the stores are open on Christmas Eve."

Burt walked into the room and stopped close by her. He was holding Ted out toward her.

"I need to take a shower," he explained as she looked at him in surprise.

There was probably no innuendo intended, but in spite of herself, Charlene felt her face growing warm. She took the baby from him and started for the door. When she glanced over her shoulder before starting on down the hall, she saw that he was standing there by the bed, looking at it. Before he could say anything more, she fled.

That evening everything was the same on the surface. Burt played with Ted on the carpet in the den, he and Charlene watched the afternoon news on television and he barbecued steaks for dinner. No mention was made of the new bedroom furnishings, but something new in the atmosphere between them quickened her heartbeat everytime her eyes collided with his. Her odd nervousness intensified while he was helping her clear the table and stack the dishes in the dishwasher.

"I'll go and check on Ted," she said when they were finished.

"No, let me."

He caught her by the shoulders and gently turned her in the direction of the den.

She caught her breath in surprise at this unexpected physical contact. The touch of his hands awoke longings that made it difficult not to lean back against him.

In the den she sat in her usual place at one end of the sofa. He was gone so long she began to wonder if he had decided to go on to bed without telling her good night, but then he did return and, instead of sitting in his preferred chair, came over and sat next to her. Her heart lurched and then raced excitedly as he picked up her hand.

"Your 'surprise' that went all wrong today, Charly. What exactly did you have in mind?" he asked in a voice that gave her not the first clue of what he was thinking.

She caught her bottom lip in her teeth, her dark eyes searching his features in desperation for some encouragement. Here it was, that moment of confrontation she had been awaiting for weeks with a mixture of hope and trepidation. Either he still found her sexually attractive or he didn't. As much as she dreaded hearing the truth, it would be better than the uncertainty.

"I should think that was fairly obvious . . . what I had in mind," she said, dropping her gaze. Having to come right out and spell out her intentions was even more excruciatingly awkward than being caught in the middle of trying to make up that damned bed. "I still find you physically attractive . . ."

While she searched her blank mind for words, his free hand came over and cupped her cheek, forcing her to turn her head and look at him.

"Are you saying that you want me to make love to you?" he asked bluntly, his tone betraying nothing of his own feelings about that prospect.

"Yes."

The admission was little more than a whisper. Her lashes dropped to cover her eyes since she couldn't turn her head aside with his hand still holding her cheek. "But only if you want to."

The last words weren't audible because he was speaking her name aloud, his voice halfway between a sigh and a groan.

"Charly."

Then he was folding her into his arms and kissing her, removing all doubts of any reluctance on his part toward touching her. His lips claimed hers with the old, urgent hunger she remembered so well, and her mouth parted willingly as his tongue came searching for the clinging sweetness of hers.

"Oh, Burt!" she groaned, pulling her lips apart from his when she was desperate for air in her lungs. Tightening her arms around his neck, she turned her face into his neck and murmured, "It's been so long! Everything is going so *fast* for me!"

"I know!" he muttered, his hands moving urgently over her shoulders and back as though he were searching out all the fine bones supporting her feminine frame.

When he gathered her into his arms and stood up, she clung to him unquestioningly. It mattered not where they went, to her bedroom or to his, only that they consummate this raging passion melting her flesh and bones and turning her into molten lava. Her whole body trembled with a strange ague.

To her surprise he carried her into the big master bedroom, and she saw, lifting her head from his shoulder, why he had taken so long when he went to check on Ted some minutes ago. The top sheet was spread neatly over the mattress and tucked under the sides. The pillows had been placed inside their cases at the head of the bed.

As he stood her on her feet next to the bed, she stared at it and then up at him.

"If you already *knew,* why did you make me *tell* you—" she asked protestingly.

"I had to be sure," he said simply. His hands curved around her waist but his passion was held in check now. It was as though he waited for her to make the next move.

"You mean you weren't sure whether it was all right for me to have intercourse?" she persisted. The last thing she really wanted was to stand here now and carry on a discussion—of *any* kind, but they had to clear up the misconceptions that stood between them.

"That, too," he said, his honest blue gaze completing the communication he didn't put into words. As difficult as she found it to believe, Burt was telling her he hadn't known whether she wanted *him!* And she thought she had been so obvious all along.

Closing her eyes, Charlene expelled a sigh from deep inside her. So much time had been wasted when they could have been enjoying each other! Opening her eyes again, she let her gaze wander appreciatively over the planes of his face, the hard jawline, the firmly molded mouth. Her hands slid across his shoulders and down his chest, not to tease him, but just to give herself the sensual joy of touching him.

"I've wanted you to make love to me for months," she said in a heartfelt voice. "But I was afraid you might not be interested. After Ted was born, you never seemed to want to touch me at all."

His hands tightened at her waist in a reflexive movement and then came up to frame her face. The rapid pulsing of blood in his fingers told her he wasn't as calm as he appeared.

"Make love to me . . . *please,*" she murmured as he brought his mouth to hers and all conversation ended. The kiss rekindled the hotness of their passion. When Burt began to undress her, she helped him, impatient to be rid of the clothes that separated them. Then he tore off his own clothes, throwing them aside, and hugged her to him, shudders of need rippling through his hard, masculine frame.

As she lay back on the enormous new bed and looked up into his face as he braced himself over her, a totally unexpected thought brought a frown of consternation to her features.

"What's wrong?" he asked quickly, going tense.

"I just happened to think—I'm not taking any precautions against getting pregnant. It could happen again."

His features relaxed.

"Do you want me to stop?"

"No."

She caught his shoulders and pulled him toward her as she spoke this unhesitating reply. He lowered his body to hers and entered her slowly and carefully, carrying the first penetration so deep that she cried out with the overwhelming pleasure of it. Moving her hips under him, she slid her hands along the ridged muscles of his back, down to his buttocks, taut and hard as molded steel. Clutching him, she urged him to thrust faster and harder and deeper, not to be so gentle. She was not a fragile thing that would break, as he seemed to fear. Her agony and her unbearable pleasure mounted and expanded until the ache inside her pelvis exploded and her head was filled with a kaleidoscope of brilliant colors.

The words she murmured as he slumped on top of her made no particular sense. Encircling the relaxed heaviness of his frame with her arms, she hugged him tight against her, feeling the warm dampness of their perspiration. The rise to climax had been explosively fast for him as well as for her, a fact that encouraged her to hope that he hadn't been satisfying his sexual needs with someone else.

After a few moments, he rolled over beside her, keeping one arm around her waist and drawing her up close to his still-warm body. She brought one hand up and stroked his cheek and the hard line of his jaw. As he turned his face into her palm and kissed it, she felt an enormous lump materialize in her throat and had to fight an unexpected threat of tears. This onslaught of emotion both surprised and puzzled her. She could explain it only as part of the aftermath of passion.

After a while she pulled free of his encircling arm with the greatest reluctance and went into the adjoining bathroom. When she came back out, she didn't know whether he would still be there or not, but he lay almost exactly as she had left him. After arranging the spread at the foot of the bed so that they could pull it up later if they needed it, she lay next to him again, sliding under the arm he lifted up and snuggling close to him.

It was silly of her, but she fought sleep, not wanting to drop off and awaken later to find herself alone in the bed. She just knew that he would slip away to his own bed before the night was over. Listening to his breathing, slow and regular, she thought he was asleep and sighed.

"What's wrong? Can't you sleep?" His voice, slurred with sleepiness, startled her.

She hesitated and then worked up her nerve.

"Burt, would you sleep in here with me . . . all night?" she asked wistfully.

He turned away from her on his side, and her heart squeezed with disappointment. She wished now she had let well enough alone.

"Sure, why not?" he said in the same half-asleep

voice. "This bed's big enough for half a dozen more . . ."

Charlene smiled in the darkness, turning over so that her body fit against his, but not *too* closely. He wasn't used to sleeping with someone. She didn't want him to feel crowded.

With this reassurance that he wouldn't be slipping off in the middle of the night, she was so sleepy she couldn't keep her eyelids up. *Why did she feel as though she had won some kind of major battle?* she wondered, as she drifted off.

Burt didn't go to the boatyard during the next two days. Charlene would look back upon the Christmas holiday immediately following it and reflect that it had been one of the happiest in her memory, with only one sad moment, occurring when she telephoned Cappy to wish him a merry Christmas. If he could have been there with them in Florida, everything would have been perfect.

And yet she hadn't attended a single party!

A couple of weeks before Christmas Burt had been sorting through the mail and noticed the invitation to the big Christmas Eve dinner-dance at the clubhouse.

"Would you like to go to this?" he had asked unexpectedly, taking her by surprise.

"No," she had answered without stopping to consider. "But if *you'd* like to go, we can."

He had dropped the subject, and instead they had spent a quiet Christmas Eve at home. After Ted had gone to sleep that evening, they turned out all the lights in the den except those on the Christmas tree.

"It *is* a beautiful tree, isn't it," Charlene mused, sitting down on the carpet next to the hassock on which Burt's feet, clad only in his socks, rested. She rested her forearm across his legs, gazing curiously at some of the presents underneath the tree. Several of them had *her* name on them.

"You can open them tonight if you like," Burt offered with a note of teasing in his voice. "This will be the last year, though. Next year Santa Claus will have to come."

"Well, maybe *one* package," Charlene conceded, succumbing to the power of temptation. "Cappy always let me open one package on Christmas Eve. Which one?"

Burt got up from his chair and went over to the tree to pick out a small package wrapped in shimmering gold with a red velvet bow. Handing it to her, he sat down on the carpet next to her to watch her open the gift.

She shook it first and went through the ritual of speculating about what could be inside it. Inwardly she was suffused with happiness at the relaxed intimacy between the two of them. Yesterday morning she had been too nervous for words waiting for that bedroom set to be delivered and wondering what Burt's reaction to it would be.

After ripping off the paper, she saw immediately that the box bore a jeweler's name. Maybe Burt had bought her a wedding ring! She wore the gold band from the set Paul had given her, having put the engagement ring away in her jewelry case.

But the present wasn't a ring. It was a diamond

solitaire pendant on a delicate gold chain, the diamond a large one and breathtakingly beautiful. Charlene stared down at it, overwhelmed that he had bought her a present so obviously expensive.

"It's beautiful," she said softly, "but I can't help saying the usual—'you shouldn't have.'"

"Do you like it?"

Looking up at him, her eyes widened with surprise at the uncertainty in his voice.

"*Like* it! I love it!"

She took the pendant out of the box and put it around her neck, allowing him to fasten it for her. The little feather kiss he planted at her nape awoke a tremor of response.

"Now I'll be embarrassed to have you open your presents from me," she said ruefully. "I feel like a cheapskate."

He slid his arms around her waist and hugged her back against him, then pushed her down on the carpet on her back, sprawling beside her on his stomach, the upper part of his body raised as he propped himself on his elbows.

"You mean I haven't already gotten my present?" Except for a telltale glint in his eyes, he might have been serious. "I thought the bed was it."

Charlene could tell he was remembering yesterday afternoon when he had discovered her sitting on the unmade bed, swathed in the ill-fitting sheet and consumed with frustration. She was still embarrassed whenever she thought of it, but at least everything had turned out well eventually.

"The bedroom set wasn't exactly a *present*," she

protested sheepishly, expectation rising as he leaned over and kissed her on the lips, gently at first, his lips exploratory and clinging. But she made a provocative invitation with the tip of her tongue as she slid it along the moist closure of his mouth and he responded immediately, deepening the kiss and searching out her impudent tongue with his own.

As he kissed her, his hands unbuttoned her blouse and dealt with the snap and front zipper of her jeans. She allowed him to undress her, lying there and looking at the passion growing on the face she found so attractive in its quiet ruggedness. In short time she was wearing nothing but the diamond pendant.

"Here! Let me!" she said as he reached for the top button on his cotton chambray shirt. She got up on her knees, and took her time about unbuttoning his shirt, feeling his eyes on her body as she directed her attention to her task. Once before she had undressed him like this, on his boat in the marina in Madisonville. Now, as then, she took pleasure in the sight of his nudity and was delighted in her power to arouse him beyond his control.

"Tease," he growled, grabbing her by the waist and falling backward, dragging her on top of him.

For just a second, she was about to protest, but then she thrust aside the vague hint of something like uneasiness. He had called her a tease that other night and later they had gotten into that disturbing discussion about all women being sorceresses at heart. But that was a long time ago. Things were changed between her and Burt now.

Lying on top of him, she could feel the unmistakable evidence of his desire pressing against her, and she moved her hips suggestively as she lowered her mouth to kiss him. His hands caressed the length of her back and molded her hips and buttocks, pulling her tighter against him.

When they both were breathless from kissing, she turned her face aside, her chest heaving and her pulses drumming with her excitement. Giving in to a bold impulse, she slid down further and planted a trail of kisses down his chest, pausing to bite his nipples. Hearing and feeling his sharply indrawn breath, she continued downward, brushing her lips against the tautness of his stomach and then lower, finding her own erotic pleasure in the intimate explorations of her tongue and mouth.

His hands soon grasped her shoulders and pulled her up to him again. His intentions were plain when he lifted her by the waist and lowered her onto his body. Charlene found the position strange at first, but she was soon enjoying the pleasure of controlling the rhythm of their lovemaking, and found it was stimulating to have Burt gaze at her body as he was doing, as though the sight of it heightened his arousal. His hands caressed her and then as she moved her hips with greater urgency, he grasped them, slowing the spiraling ascent of their passion and making the pleasure more excruciating in its intensity.

At the moment of climax, she felt her body go rigid and then was unable to move for several seconds as the weakness invaded all her bones and joints. Murmuring words that somehow expressed her sense of wonder at the cataclysmic pleasure their lovemaking gave her, she leaned forward and kissed him on the lips and then collapsed on top of his chest. The tender caress of his hands on her back and shoulders was as sweet to her as the actual lovemaking had been.

The next morning when they opened the rest of the presents, Charlene was struck again by the expensiveness of Burt's gifts to her. There was a large bottle of French perfume in an exquisite crystal bottle and half a dozen smart tennis ensembles he had bought at the Atlantic Heights tennis shop.

She was a little uncertain as to how she should react to the tennis clothes. Why had he given them to her since she wasn't playing tennis?

"The woman who waited on me said you could exchange these for another size if they don't fit—or you can pick out something entirely different," he commented as she held up a lovely, pale pink velour warm-up suit in front of her. There was a skirt and blouse with accents of the same color.

Charlene kept to herself what she was thinking: *she would try to return the clothes for a refund.*

During the week between Christmas and New Year's, she had never been happier in her life. Reveling in her new physical intimacy with Burt, she took every opportunity to touch him and quite unashamedly enjoyed the sight of his body either partially clothed or completely nude. It was too good to be true that she was free to walk into the bathroom when he was toweling off from a shower. Her sexual appetite was apparently insatiable and he could arouse her with a certain expression in his eyes, even before he touched her. She had definitely become a sensual woman.

The only cloud on her mental horizon was Burt's failure to indicate his awareness that her period of separation from Paul would be over soon. At that time Paul would proceed with the necessary legal steps for divorce, as he had agreed to do, and she would be free to marry Burt.

Her hopes soared when he asked her to arrange for a babysitter for New Year's Eve. They seldom went out, and she sensed that the event was going to be an "occasion." Perhaps he was setting the stage for a "proposal," she speculated with a thrill of anticipation she recognized as ridiculous under the circumstances. They already were living as man and wife.

Instead of the quiet dinner at a nice restaurant that she had expected, it turned out that Burt had made reservations, without even consulting her, to attend the New Year's Eve party at the club. There was a lavish buffet and champagne poured freely, while an orchestra played dance music. Charlene was dumbfounded when he announced to her where they were going.

From years of having attended such affairs with Paul while they were married, she managed without much effort to appear as if she were enjoying herself. She talked and laughed with the countless couples they met, and danced with many of the men. The whole time she was surreptitiously keeping an eye on Burt and wondering if he were enjoying himself. It was difficult to tell. He was making an obvious effort to join into the social mêlée but it caused her some uneasiness that he was downing one Scotch on the rocks after another, disdaining to drink the champagne. Aside from beer, she had never seen him drink before, and he always drank that in moderation.

"Why don't we go?" she asked several times in an undertone when she could manage to get him aside.

"Aren't you having a good time?" he replied.

Sensing that he wanted her to enjoy herself, that he was quite probably just enduring this whole situation for her sake, she would answer in the affirmative and continue the pretense. It was just one night. She would try to prevent this kind of thing from happening again.

When midnight finally arrived and she danced with him to the strains of "Auld Lang Syne," she knew in spite of his carefully controlled movements that he was drunk.

"I'm ready to go home," she told him firmly. "I promised the babysitter we wouldn't be more than a few minutes past midnight."

He didn't argue. Indeed he seemed hardly aware of her. She knew from past experience that people react to an excessive amount of alcohol in various ways. Burt, not surprisingly, was one of those who sink deep into a somber silence.

The babysitter was a teen-aged girl who lived several houses away on the same street. Charlene stood outside on her driveway and watched until the girl had reached the safety of her own home. Then she went inside and found that Burt had managed to get undressed and sat slumped on the edge of the bed, his face in his hands.

"Are you nauseated?" she asked in concern, going over and placing her hand gently on his head.

". . . can't do it," he mumbled incoherently.

"You can't do what?" she asked solicitously. "Can I get you something? Some aspirin perhaps?"

There was nothing to indicate that he had heard her. It seemed to her that he was somewhere far away in a world created by his alcoholic stupor.

". . . will never work," he said with a heavy sigh.

Feeling at a loss, Charlene undressed and then went into the bathroom to brush her teeth and remove her makeup. When she came back out, Burt had managed to lie down in bed and was asleep, breathing heavily. She stood beside the bed and looked down at him, stirred deeply by tenderness and concern and an aching regret that New Year's Eve, the beginning of a new year as well as the end of an old one, had been like this. What a terrible disappointment the whole evening had been. She had so hoped for something entirely different.

The next day she was understanding when Burt awoke with a tremendous hangover and showed little interest in either food or conversation. He lay on the sofa much of the day staring at the television screen, which was dominated the entire day by football games. But if she made some comment about a certain play or asked him a question, his response made her wonder if he were really following the action. Once it was on the tip of her tongue to tease him with the gibe, "All-American husband!" but then she held the words back.

Foolishly she told herself that he would be back to normal the next day. Their *relationship* would be back to normal. But unbeknownst to her, everything had changed, and she didn't have a clue as to the reason. One day followed another, and Burt was distant and unapproachable.

"What's wrong?" she kept asking at first.

"Nothing," he would answer.

She tried with words and gestures to get through the invisible barrier separating them, but nothing had any effect. Burt wouldn't noticeably recoil when she would touch him with casual familiarity, but there was no answering response and before long she stopped making the overtures.

They still slept in the same bed, but that was different, too. Their lovemaking was infrequent now and was like something Burt did against his will. Charlene no longer felt she could initiate sexual foreplay and her hurt and confusion kept her from responding with her former lack of inhibition.

Throughout the first half of January, her mind kept going back to the New Year's Eve party and that puzzling scene afterwards. Something must have happened that night to bring about the change in Burt, but she had no inkling of what it had been. And he obviously did not intend to tell her.

Another change caused her considerable distress. Burt came home from the boatyard late now and left the house on most weekend days as well, explaining briefly that work had piled up at the boatyard.

Charlene knew intuitively that he was just staying away from the house as much as possible.

As a result of the New Year's Eve party, the telephone rang with a new frequency and there were invitations from people they had met at the party. At first, she would ask Burt if he would like to go to a dinner party at a neighbor's house or to an outdoor barbecue, whatever the invitation happened to be. But after several times when she saw his negative reaction and the apparent conflict it caused him to admit he wasn't interested, she simply refused the invitations on her own.

Also as a result of the party, where she had talked tennis enough for the news to circulate that she had once played competitive club tennis, she received an influx of invitations to play tennis. One evening just as they were about to finish dinner, the telephone rang and answering it, she found her caller to be another woman urging her to come out to the courts the following morning for Women's Day so that she could meet all the regular club players.

"It's so nice of you to ask me, Betty," she said, launching into her polite refusal. "I haven't played in a year. I'm sure I wouldn't be able to hit the ball . . ." She had to wait while Betty put in reassurances to the effect that "it all comes back." Charlene glanced over at Burt and was struck by his attentiveness to the conversation. He seemed to be waiting for her to continue as though eager for her final decision. It was so rare lately for him to indicate any interest in anything in her presence that she decided on impulse to accept the invitation just to get his reaction. He had urged her strongly to get involved in tennis when they first moved into the house, and at Christmas he had bought her those expensive tennis outfits. Maybe she would please him if she began to play again.

"If you're sure you won't mind taking a chance on me, Betty, I'll come out tomorrow at ten," she put in when given the chance to speak. "Thanks for calling me."

Without being too obvious, she watched Burt's face as she spoke these words and saw a strong element of satisfaction mixed with what appeared to be *relief*. Why he should react in that particular way she could not fathom. But if it were important to him that she play tennis, then play tennis she would.

With a maid coming in once a week to help with the housecleaning and Burt away at the boatyard most of his waking hours, she did have time on her hands. Ted was a good baby and didn't require constant attention and, besides, conversation with him had its limitations. Tennis would help take up her time and perhaps the exercise would help her vent her unhappiness.

As January passed and Charlene found herself a divorced woman, she agreed to more and more tennis dates and began playing bridge two mornings a week. Against all her intentions, she was becoming involved in the country club life again, but she had to do something to fill the hours and to keep herself from thinking.

A hundred times she almost broached the subject of her divorce with Burt, but somehow she never could force the words out. She would practice various approaches, ranging from the offhanded to something straight from the heart, which would reveal how hurt she was inside, but pride kept her from speaking. Part of the time, anger was mixed in liberal portions with the pride.

Didn't Burt realize what an insufferably awkward position he had placed her in? Conscience required that she return Paul's accumulated alimony payments if she were going to continue being supported in high style by Burt, and yet how could she relinquish her security with no promise of marriage?

In weak moments she thought longingly of those idyllic months of her pregnancy when she had lived with Burt in the little stucco house and walked nearly every day to the boatyard. She had loved the feeling of being included in his work world. After some deep soul-searching, it seemed to her that he hadn't wanted her to be a part of that world. Why else would he have bought this too-large house located at a considerable distance from the boatyard and then pressed her to become involved in club activities? When she had steadfastly resisted, he had taken her to the New Year's Eve dance and seen to it that she met all those people and subsequently found herself deluged with tennis invitations.

But what she couldn't explain to herself was what Burt was getting personally out of this whole deal. He was going to enormous expense for just a few hours with his son, since he spent so little time at home anymore. Maybe he had realized his mistake in bringing her to Florida and was hoping she would divine his wishes and take herself off his hands. But it was awfully unfair of him not to tell her outright.

By mid-February she had begun to find her situation intolerable. The silence between herself and Burt on all the important issues seemed to breed even more silence, and her misery grew. She decided to take Ted to Louisiana to visit Cappy. Perhaps at the marina she could get some badly needed perspective and decide what to do next. She didn't think she could continue living with Burt in Florida, considering the way things were between them.

Awakening early on a Saturday morning, she discovered that Burt was gone from the bed and wondered with a pang of dismay if he had already left the house for the day. *This just can't go on,* she reflected dully, getting up and slipping on her robe.

But he hadn't gone yet. He was in the den with Ted, who was fussing and showing little inclination to drink the bottle Burt had prepared. In spite of her increased involvement in club activities, Charlene had continued to nurse him. It wasn't that difficult to manage since he needed to be fed about every three hours once he was past the stage of early infancy, and if necessary he could take a formula in a bottle. But he much preferred his mother's natural method of feeding him.

"He's hungry," she said unnecessarily, venturing into the room without knowing if she were welcome or not. These days she was never quite sure of anything where Burt was concerned.

"I tried to talk him into being quiet so that his mother could sleep, but he wouldn't listen to reason," Burt said after a quick glance at her, directing the gently chiding words to the baby who was working up to full crying volume at the sound of Charlene's voice.

She took the baby and sat on the sofa to nurse him. In seconds he was quiet and sucking with noisy contentment at her breast. Burt watched in silence for a brief time and then got to his feet and began to walk out of the room.

"Burt, could I talk to you?" she said quickly, wanting to tell him of her decision to visit Cappy before he left the house and was gone for the rest of the day.

"Sure," he said from the doorway, not turning around. "Just let me get another cup of coffee. Would you like one, too?"

"Please." Nervousness made her voice slightly hoarse and she cleared her throat, unfortunately deepening the sense of drama she hadn't wanted to create in the first place.

When he returned with the two mugs of coffee, he placed hers on the end table within her reach and sat down in a chair, appearing anything but relaxed.

"What was it you wanted to tell me?" he said, coming immediately to the point.

Painfully aware of the great distance separating them, she lowered her gaze to the baby she held cradled in her arms and lightly stroked the down softness of his head.

"I've been thinking it's about time Cappy got to know his great-grandson," she said as naturally as she could, feeling as miserable as she did. Lifting her head, she caught the expression on Burt's face and for a moment was stirred by the wild hope that he was going to refuse to let them go. He looked positively stricken! But then almost immediately the pain was gone from his eyes and his features, and he was making inquiries into her plans in a voice lacking any emotion whatsoever, not even curiosity.

"When are you planning to leave?"

"In a day or two. I haven't talked to Cappy about it yet. I wanted to check with you first."

Now that she had actually stated her intention to go to Louisiana, she was having severe second thoughts about leaving. Maybe if she just remained patient a while longer, he would tell her what was wrong. All it would take from him was the slightest hint that he would miss her, and she wouldn't go.

"How long do you plan to stay?"

From his tone she might have been going next door for a Tupperware party. His apparent indifference so overwhelmed Charlene with a sense of hopelessness that temporarily she found it impossible to think of what she would do for the rest of the day, let alone the following weeks and months.

"I don't know," she said listlessly.

"I see." He sat utterly still, apparently digesting her answer and showing no reaction to its inconclusiveness. When he spoke again, she guessed he must have been going over the practical considerations in his mind.

"Are you going to fly to New Orleans?"

She swallowed hard at the lump in her throat and

made a tremendous effort to match his own matter-of-factness.

"I thought I'd drive. That way I'll have my car when I get there. Ted loves to ride in his car seat, and . . . it doesn't really matter how long it takes us to get there." Not since he didn't care that they were going and probably didn't wish for them to return, she might have added, but didn't, keeping to the rules of this polite exchange.

Her reply drew a reflexive response so fleeting she wasn't sure she hadn't imagined it. His features had seemed to constrict in a little spasm, but then he looked calm and unmoved again.

"You could fly and pick up a rental car at the airport," he pointed out thoughtfully, but even as he made the suggestion, she knew he wouldn't argue, no matter what she decided. It was as though mentally he had already made the adjustment to her being gone from his life. She probably had been a part of it only in her imagination, only in her deep longing. As much credit as she had to give him for trying, as evidenced by all the money he had spent and his acceding to her wishes by sharing a bedroom with her, he simply hadn't been able in the final analysis to relinquish the necessity for solitude and privacy. He had tried to fit himself into the role of married man and found it wouldn't work for him. As soon as she was gone, he would return to being a loner.

Thoughts of his generosity to her and the firm perception of his essential goodness as a human being sustained Charlene through the remainder of that day and the next as she made preparations for her trip. How could she feel bitter against Burt for what he could not help?

If she had ventured to hope that her imminent leave-taking would cause Burt to spend most of that weekend at home, she was sadly disappointed, for he was gone most of Saturday and Sunday. On Monday, the day she was to leave, she arose to find that he had already left the house. It was a bitter realization that he hadn't even wanted to say good-bye to her and Ted.

She drove the interstates, finding their endless monotony appropriate for her state of mind. Ted was even better than she had dared hope, and she made the drive in three days. On the way she thought of another trip to Madisonville by car, her trip from Atlanta just a little more than a year ago now, her separation from Paul fresh in her mind. So much had happened to her during the interval between that trip and this one. She didn't seem like the same person to herself. How ironic it was that she was much more upset now at the prospect of being separated from Burt than she had been knowing her husband was living with another woman and her marriage of ten years was on the rocks.

Cappy was happy to see her and made a great fuss over Ted. Charlene's spirits were buoyed temporarily upon her arrival, but when two days passed and Burt didn't telephone, her depression returned. Surely he must know she would have arrived by now. Wasn't he at least concerned about his son, if not about her? For Cappy's sake, she tried hard to put up a front, but he knew her too well and with a characteristic forthrightness posed the questions that had to be answered eventually.

"It ain't workin' out with you and Burt, is it, Charly?" he said on the evening of her third day at the marina.

"No, Cappy, it isn't," she admitted unhappily.

He frowned and fidgeted with his pipe. Intuition told her he wasn't comfortable with the subject he was about to broach.

"What do you and Burt plan to do about making little Ted . . . legal?" he asked finally. "You ain't made no mention of the two of you gettin' married like you said you was going to do after you got your divorce. You got it now, don't you?"

Charlene was careful not to sound critical of Burt as she answered Cappy's question at some length, even though deep inside her she did think Burt hadn't acted fairly toward her when he failed to state openly his intentions in regard to marriage—or rather his lack of them.

"I guess Burt must have found out marriage wasn't for him, Cappy," she concluded.

"What you're telling me just don't sound like the Burt I know," Cappy stated emphatically. "He ain't the kind to go back on his word like that. Are you certain he knows *you're* wantin' to go through with marryin' *him*?"

"He must know," she said with a conviction that

made him sit for a long while, mulling over the situation she had explained and shaking his head in puzzlement from time to time.

"Something's wrong here," he said finally and got up to go off to bed.

The positiveness of Cappy's reaction awakened in Charlene the glimmer of a hope. Maybe there was a simple explanation she had overlooked. *Had* Burt been unsure of her willingness to marry him? Or maybe she had exaggerated in her own mind his standoffishness with her. On impulse she went to the telephone and dialed the number of the house in Florida. The hour's time difference made it almost midnight, and Burt would more than likely be asleep by now, but she urgently needed to talk to him while she had the nerve.

A full two minutes later she hung up the phone, unable to believe what was clearly evident. Burt wasn't home. Where could he be at this late hour?

For the first time there occurred a possibility she hadn't considered before now. Was Burt involved with another woman? Was that the reason he was so distant with her? All her instincts shouted a loud negative answer to those questions. *No! It wasn't true!*

In Paul's case, she had registered a number of telltale signs on a subconscious level so that the truth hadn't taken her by surprise when it finally came and she learned he was having an affair with another woman. But she just *knew* Burt wasn't capable of anything cheap and clandestine. He was too forthright and honest. But where *was* he at this hour of the night, then?

Charlene went to bed, but found herself unable to sleep. At one-hour intervals she got up and went to the telephone in the kitchen, being very quiet so as not to disturb Cappy. Just before dawn she gave up all hope, unequivocally sure that Burt was spending the night somewhere else besides their house. But *where?* And *with whom?*

The following afternoon Cappy unwittingly brought matters to a head when he brought up another question that obviously had been bothering him.

"You plan to take Ted over to let Ed and Inez Landry get a look at their grandson?" His tone was more gravelly than usual out of apology, as if he were uncomfortably aware even as he asked that the matter was none of his business.

With no warning Charlene burst into tears.

"I don't know what to do, Cappy!" she managed to get out between gulping sobs.

He blinked and looked at her with a mixture of dismay and apprehension, not comprehending how his query could bring on that much emotional tumult. Burt's parents might not approve of the circumstances under which little Ted had come into the world, but they knew about him. They were church-going people and apt to be "cut and dried" in their moral code, as Cappy acknowledged himself to be, too, but Burt's son would mean something special to them. Knowing all this, Cappy had had to ask when days went by and Charlene had made no mention of seeing them.

"Didn't Burt say anything—?" he began and then broke off when he saw there was nothing to do but wait until Charlene had calmed down enough to speak.

The restive quality of Cappy's silence and the sight of his distress through the blur of her tears helped Charlene get a grip upon her emotions. She was being dreadfully unfair to him, subjecting him to her breakdown, which was the result of last night's sleeplessness and anxiety as much as anything else. Cappy's question had been the catalyst.

"The subject never came up," she said when she managed to speak. "I told Burt a week ago today I was coming here to visit you, and I must not have seen him more than two or three hours the whole weekend. Besides that, there were so many . . . *other* things on my mind, I have to admit I didn't even ask him if he wanted me to take Ted over to his parents' house, and he didn't bring up the subject himself."

"I reckon you could *call* him." Cappy's hesitancy said he was highly uncomfortable with all this female emotion and was afraid to say anything now for fear of tripping it off again.

Charlene held her breath a moment, determined to hold back the fresh onslaught of tears.

"I can try," she said in a small, tight voice, on the verge of telling Cappy of her efforts to call Burt last night. But hadn't she worried Cappy enough with her problems?

They were sitting at the kitchen table. Cappy had come into the house for an afternoon cup of coffee, and Ted was taking a nap, innocent of his place at the center of this emotional storm.

"I reckon I'll just call him myself," Cappy announced grimly, rising abruptly from the table and going over to the wall telephone. "I need to talk to Burt and get some things straight—"

Charlene watched him as he picked up the directory from the shelf beneath the telephone and turned it over to see the numbers he had written on the back. She could have recited the number of her house for him, but she didn't, keeping quiet and waiting with a sense of inevitability. As she expected, Cappy got no answer at the house. When he dialed *one* and then another ten-digit number, her heart beat faster with dread. He was calling the boatyard! Burt might be there, even at this time of day on Saturday. Dear God, she hoped she wouldn't be the cause of bad feeling between Cappy and Burt! That complication hadn't occurred to her before just now.

After what seemed to her an interminable period of time, Cappy hung up the phone, his face wreathed in a frown that contained worry as well as impatience and grim determination.

"Reckon I'll go on out to the store," was all he said.

Charlene knew it was useless to point out that he didn't need to tend the store and the fuel dock today. It was a miserable winter day with the north wind whistling around the corners of the house and a drizzling rain that threatened to turn into sleet as the temperature dropped closer to freezing. This year, February in Louisiana wasn't mild and springlike the way it had been last year. People weren't out on the river today, even though it was Saturday.

Most of them were probably at home with their families, Charlene reflected with a stab of guilt as she watched Cappy put on his watch cap and shrug into his jacket. It was the kind of day one could enjoy staying inside with the tantalizing aroma of freshly baked bread coming from the kitchen and a big pot of soup simmering on the back burner for supper. She could be providing those pleasures for her grandfather if she weren't so miserable herself, so plagued with the problems she had brought here and heaped upon his old shoulders. It had been thoughtless of her to come under the present circumstances. Her visit wasn't a joy to him. It was a trial and a worry.

In Florida she had formulated the plans for her trip, hoping that in Madisonville, where she had spent her happy growing-up years, she might gain some perspective on her life. Well, she had arrived at one decision, at least. Whatever direction her life took, she couldn't keep in the back of her mind the possibility of coming back here and living with Cappy. She had to kill this fledgling instinct to return to the warm security of the nest. She was no helpless girl, but a mature woman with a child. Her problems and her responsibilities were her own—not Cappy's. He deserved to live out his old age in peace, puttering happily around his marina and store, relieved of the actual physical work now that he had hired a full-time employee, a cousin of Burt's who displayed an avid interest in the marina and hung on to Cappy's every word as Burt himself had once done.

Burt had pointed out to her last July in Atlanta that it wouldn't be fair of her to go back to Madisonville to have her baby. He had known what she had just realized. She wouldn't be surprised at all to learn that he had been the one responsible for Cappy's hiring someone to help him.

As she rinsed the coffee cups after Cappy had left the house, Charlene gazed out the window over the sink. The scene before her eyes was gray and blurred by the misty rain, but familiar to her in this somber guise as well as in so many others. In her heart of hearts, this marina would always occupy that special place, *home*. It was saddening and a little frightening, too, to realize she couldn't come here and lay her problems at Cappy's doorstep and "live happily ever after," in the way of childish fantasy, but at the same time she felt stronger now, more resolute, perhaps finally mature.

That afternoon she made two telephone calls, one long distance to Atlanta and the other local. Over dinner she told Cappy of her plans to return to Florida on Monday.

"It's supposed to be clearing up tomorrow. I hope we have good weather for driving Monday," she said matter-of-factly, as though that emotional scene this afternoon had never occurred and she was simply returning home after her visit was completed.

Cappy put down his fork and looked at her, sadness at the thought of her leaving in his old, lined face, but other emotions as well, approval and unmistakable pride.

"I'm real glad to hear that," he said gruffly.

They both knew his meaning. He wasn't talking about the weather and he could never be *glad* she was leaving. He loved her too much for that. But somehow he had sensed the change in her and was pleased with her new independence.

"Tomorrow afternoon Ted and I are supposed to go over to Burt's folks' house for coffee and cake," she said, trying not to give a hint of her reservations about that visit. Her conversation with Inez Landry this afternoon had been stiff with reticence on both sides. Charlene didn't look forward to confronting Burt's parents, knowing they couldn't possibly approve of her. "Mrs. Landry invited you, too," she added a trifle hopefully.

Satisfaction softened the black piercing quality of Cappy's eyes. Something akin to a smile tugged at his lips.

"That woman makes a good cake," he declared heartily. "Don't know as I could pass up that invitation."

And then he and Charlene were looking at each other for an emotion-charged moment during which they communicated all that was left unsaid. *I'm behind you, girl, in this and everything else,* Cappy was saying. *Thanks, Cappy. Not just for your support in this one instance, but for what you've been to me my whole life . . . for what you are*, she was telling him in return.

"Here," Charlene said aloud, blinking to relieve the hot prickling of tears. "Somebody's going to have to eat this last little helping of mashed potatoes."

"Don't mind if I do," Cappy said, taking the bowl from her and blinking, too, as he scraped the contents into his plate. "I'm spoiled rotten with all this good cooking."

Charlene had time for extended reflection on the drive back to Florida and concluded that she couldn't regret having made the trip after all. There had been painful moments for herself and Cappy, too, but they had parted with a new relationship. She had gained his respect and his confidence. Knowing that he believed she would be able to handle her problems with Burt bolstered her own faith in herself.

When she turned into the driveway of the house in Atlantic Heights late Wednesday afternoon, nervousness quickened her pulse and created a heavy sensation in her midriff. She was back now. There was reality to face. It remained to be seen if one of those scenes she had worked out in her mind, all of them with happy endings, would actually occur.

Burt wasn't home, but then she hadn't expected him to be. The house was precisely as she had left it. He might never have come back at all after he had left it early that Monday morning.

Ted was fretful, tired, hungry and demanding her attention. Charlene nursed him before she took the time to do anything else. He fell asleep at her breast.

After she had lain him in his bed in the nursery, she dialed the number of the boatyard. There was no answer. It was six o'clock by now and everyone should have gone home, but she had wanted to make sure Burt wasn't there, working late, before she tried to locate him elsewhere.

Now what? she asked herself. Should she try calling one of his employees, Cindy being the obvious first choice? But what if it turned out none of them knew where Burt was staying? She would have aroused all kinds of curiosity on their part, and Burt would hate that. He was such a private person—

Suddenly she was struck with force by a possibility she hadn't considered before. Quickly she picked up the telephone receiver and dialed.

"Hello," came his low, familiar voice, terse and annoyed as though he hadn't expected a call and would have little patience with the person who had disturbed him.

Charlene gripped the receiver tighter, her fingers trembling, unable to say anything for a moment.

"Hello. Who the hell *is* this?" he demanded curtly and then hung up none too gently, the sharp click making her start.

For a second her finger was poised to dial again, but she hung up the receiver instead and got out the directory to look up the number of the teen-aged girl she usually hired to babysit with Ted. Luckily the girl was home and agreed to come over within a few minutes.

Burt's pickup was parked underneath the carport of the little stucco house. Charlene pulled her car up behind it, her nervousness having grown to full-flown proportions now that she was actually going to face him and force an end to the silence. Tonight everything was going to come out into the open, whatever the final outcome.

She still had her keys to the house, but it wouldn't be fair just to walk in on him without warning when he didn't even know she had returned to Florida. With this in mind, she slammed the door of her car and walked up to the door leading from the carport into the kitchen, where she knocked on one of the glass panes. After an interminable wait, she knocked again, the suspense suffocating. When Burt still didn't appear, she tried the door and found that it wasn't even locked. The doorknob turned easily under her hand.

"Burt!" she called as she stepped inside the kitchen, feeling like an intruder until she began to look around her.

The old dinette set was back in its former place. Indeed, the kitchen looked exactly as it had before! When she bought the new set for the breakfast room in the Atlantic Heights house, he had simply brought the old furniture back here, without telling her!

The living room was exactly as it had been before, too, the furniture arranged the way it had been when she saw it the first time, the way it had been when she went off to the hospital to give birth to Ted. The television set was playing, but otherwise there was no sign of Burt.

Charlene stood in the open archway gazing about her with a deepening sense of betrayal. The truth was dawning and with it faded away all her hope and the store of confidence she had built during the past three days when she drove across four states to get back here to him.

"Charly!"

The stunned ejaculation came from the doorway across the room that led into the hall. A glance at Burt told her why he hadn't been aware of her presence before now. Evidently he had been in the shower. His hair was wet and he wore nothing but jeans, his torso and his feet bare.

Recovering from the first paralyzing effects of discovering her there in the living room, he walked swiftly across the room, stopping in front of her and grasping her by the shoulders.

"Has something happened to Ted?" he demanded harshly, his fingers biting painfully into her flesh. When she didn't answer, merely continued to stare into his face with bleak accusation and pain, he shook her roughly. "Answer me! What's wrong?"

"Ted's fine. He's at . . . the other house asleep, with a sitter. Cappy's fine, too."

At the first sound of her voice, a dull, resigned monotone, his fingers went lax and then his hands fell away from her shoulders. He stared into her face questioningly, his eyes still luminous with the effects of his shock.

"You never gave it a chance, did you, Burt?" she asked bitterly, swallowing in an effort to rid herself of the big wad that had collected in her throat and was making her faintly nauseous. "I tried to tell you in Atlanta you wouldn't be able to adjust to living with someone day in and day out. Fool that I am, I let you talk me into coming here with you. I *believed* you when you said you would marry me—"

The cleanly masculine scent of him filled her nostrils, oddly accentuating her resentment and her despair, as well. Meaning to escape it, she started to move past him, but he caught her arm and stopped her.

"I don't know what you're talking about." His puzzlement was tinged with impatience and the faintest beginnings of suspicion. "I *do* want to marry you."

"You do?" She stopped trying to pull free of the hand that held her and looked searchingly into his face.

He stared back, the suspicion hardening.

"What kind of new game is this you're playing with me, Charly? You knew I wanted us to be married. I told you that in Atlanta."

"But you never mentioned it once after that," she demurred. "Not even when my separation was over and the divorce final." Relief was weakening all the joints in her body. He *did* want to marry her! That at least was something, even if he did not love her the way she had come to love him.

"I was waiting for *you* to tell me what you had decided," he rejoined sharply. "You were the one who insisted we should wait until you were free and then decide whether to get married." His face showed the struggle he underwent with pride before he added, "Having you turn me down doesn't get any easier with practice, you know."

This admission ripped her own pride into shreds, which she resolutely tossed aside. Her dark eyes implored him to believe her as she spoke. All her feelings were there in plain sight for him to see.

"I wouldn't have turned you down, Burt," she said humbly. "You have no idea of what I've been through the last few weeks, thinking you had changed your mind about wanting to marry me. You acted as though you couldn't stand being around me. You were never home. And then when I told you I was going to Louisiana to visit Cappy, you seemed so relieved to be rid of me. After I got to Cappy's and tried to call you, you weren't ever home. I thought . . . well, you can imagine what I thought— that you were with another woman.

"And then tonight I took one look at this place, and I realized the whole time I was trying to make a home for us, you were carting all the old furniture back here, fixing this place up . . . just waiting until you could move back in here and be by yourself again." Her emotions threatened to overwhelm her, but she stubbornly fought back the tears, not willing to succumb to that weakness and make the situation more painful for the both of them than it already was. Besides, she wasn't finished speaking yet.

"Then you walk in here and see me and all you can think about is . . . Ted. I was jealous of my own baby. I wanted you to be happy to see *me*." Blinking hard and swallowing, she mustered the rueful facsimile of a smile. The fingers gripping her arm had loosened gradually and were moving ever so slightly as if to soothe away the numbness they had inflicted. "Because—you want to know something really funny?" she continued. "The gal who didn't even believe in 'head-over-heels-in-love' is exactly that. I don't know when or how it happened, but I should have known something was up when I wanted to murder Cindy just because she works with you." A little break in her voice on the last word made her effort at the light touch fall flat.

Burt's free hand came up and clasped her other arm. It wasn't clear to her whether he was fending her off or keeping her from any possible attempt to escape him. His voice revealed the same ambivalence.

"I wish I could believe you. I did everything on God's earth I could think of to make you satisfied so you would stay here. But I realized that night at the New Year's Eve party that I just can't live your kind of life, Charly, no matter how hard I might try. It's not that there's anything wrong with it or with the people in Atlantic Heights and places like that. I don't look down on them or feel inferior, either. I just feel *different* and I have to be myself, live the kind of life that's right for me. Even if it means losing you." He hesitated and then the next words seemed to break free of him against his will. "I'd do anything within my power to keep you if I thought you'd be happy with me."

Charlene strained toward him involuntarily, but his hold on her arms kept her from coming any closer to him. She lifted her hands toward his chest and then dropped them.

"I never *wanted* that house or the membership in the club or any of that!" she said passionately. "You forced it all on me. I kept telling you all that time I was pregnant that I loved *this* house, but you refused to believe me. I was so happy here. I liked walking to the boatyard every day and helping out when I could. I liked having you come home for lunch every day. Couldn't you tell how disappointed I was that day you picked me up at the hospital and took me to the new house? It was hard to keep from crying, but I had to try to act appreciative since you'd already bought it. What could I say that wouldn't have hurt your feelings?"

Uncertainty showed on Burt's face. His fingers moved gently, almost caressingly, on her arms.

"I just thought I probably hadn't made a good choice," he said thoughtfully, obviously wanting to believe her and yet not totally convinced. "How long do you think you could be satisfied with me, Charly? What if in a year or five years or ten, you get bored? What then?" His blue eyes held yearning as they searched hers.

The urge to touch him was too strong now to suppress. She lifted her hands to his bare shoulders and held him as lightly as he held her.

"I love you, Burt, in a way I never loved Paul. I was never jealous of him the way I am of you. The thought of losing him never made me feel the way I felt when I came in here tonight . . . like I'd just like to die. But I can't give you any promises that nothing will ever change between us. You can't promise me that, either. Life is too uncertain. We just have to gamble on each other." She spoke the words with a simple directness, knowing that her honesty might be her complete undoing.

His fingers closed convulsively on her arms, cutting off the circulation, and then his resistance failed him and he closed his arms around her, drawing her tight against his chest.

"God, I'm glad you came back!" he breathed into her hair. "When you said you were going to visit Cappy, I thought that was just a nice way of telling me you had had enough. I didn't think you were coming back. I couldn't even make myself call you for fear you'd tell me that."

Charlene hugged him tighter around the neck and turned her face into his bare chest, pressing a kiss against the clean, soap-scented skin and feeling the thud of his heartbeat reverberate against her lips.

"If you had just given me a hint that you didn't want me to go, I wouldn't have," she confessed wistfully. "And then when you didn't even say good-bye . . ."

"I couldn't."

He burrowed his face down under her hair and began to brush his lips against her neck, awakening trembling sensations of pleasure.

"I took Ted to see your parents," she said in an abstracted tone, finding it difficult to concentrate on the things she still had to tell him.

He raised his head and held her away from him a few inches to look into her face.

"You did?"

The expression in his eyes made her thankful she had overcome all her qualms and followed the bidding of her conscience.

"Cappy went with me. It was awkward at first, but once we're married, they'll accept everything, don't you think?" With Burt's arms around her, she found her outlook on everything optimistic.

"Sure they will," he said confidently, hugging her close against him once again. "What did they think of Ted?"

The unmistakable paternal pride drew a smile from Charlene.

"Naturally they were overwhelmed by his intelligence, beauty and charm," she teased. "He drooled all over everybody without showing any discrimination. He's definitely trying to cut teeth already, you know."

Burt's hands were moving over her back and shoulders with an urgency that made her breath come more quickly as her own need rose to match his. Seeking the sensitive spot at the side of her neck with his lips again, he murmured between kisses, "I guess we should go back to the other house."

She agreed with the greatest reluctance.

"We should. I told Sally I wouldn't be gone long. She has school tomorrow."

At the back of her mind was an impulsive plan she didn't mention now. After they had ridden back to the house in Atlantic Heights in her car and sent the babysitter home, the two of them went together to check on the baby, who was still sleeping soundly.

"Why don't we take him back to the other house and spend the night there?" she suggested in a whisper. The idea was impractical as well as whimsical since they would have to devise a makeshift bed for Ted, but she wanted everything to be perfect for Burt tonight. As far as she was concerned, it didn't matter as long as they were together.

He put an arm around her shoulder and led her out of the room into the hall before answering.

"I can't wait that long to make love to you," he said huskily, kissing her with an unrestrained hunger that quickly aroused both of them to a fever pitch of passion.

Charlene decided that she couldn't wait that long either. It seemed a long walk to the bedroom.

"I love you," she said later, for the umpteenth time as she nestled contentedly in his arms, entirely satisfied. "It *feels* so good to say that," she added whimsically.

"It feels unbelievable to me to hear you say it," he said seriously, rubbing his cheekbone gently against the top of her head and cradling her even closer.

He hadn't come right out and told her in words that he loved her yet, but she knew he cared and his reticence didn't diminish her happiness. With time he would come to trust her more. She hoped eventually to remove all traces of those old scars she had inflicted.

"Burt, I wasn't completely responsible for your distrust of women, was I?" she asked remorsefully.

"Of course not," he replied unhesitatingly, bringing to life a little imp of jealousy inside her.

"Oh," she said in a small voice. "That's good." She didn't like to think about him with other women, but there had to have been a great many of them, judging from his skill at lovemaking, anyway.

"You sound disappointed," he observed, chuckling in amusement. "The truth is that I was over you in a relatively short time. It was only an infatuation anyway. I wasn't in love with you, but with an ideal I had created in my fantasies."

She remembered that he had told her something like that before, though not in such a matter-of-fact tone. She still wasn't entirely convinced.

"You sure acted like you were holding a grudge when we first ran into each other in the marina last year," she commented.

"I didn't have any desire to get involved with you, for any number of reasons," he said honestly. "But mainly because I assumed that basically you hadn't changed since high school, and you as much as told me that yourself, if you remember."

"Once a cheerleader, always a cheerleader," she mused ruefully.

"Exactly," he confirmed with a ruthless candor that made her wince.

"What made you change your mind?" When he didn't answer at once, she added imploringly, "You *did* change your mind, I trust?"

"I was tempted to think I had been wrong when you pitched in and helped out while Cappy was in the hospital. But I told myself you were just entertained by the novelty of a new situation and temporarily at loose ends since your husband had walked out on you. I guess the thing that really threw me was your attitude about being pregnant. I expected you to hate it, and you didn't. Then after you came here to Florida, you were such a good sport about everything . . . and so goddamned beautiful."

"Beautiful!" she echoed in disbelief, remembering how ungainly she had become during those last months of pregnancy.

"Beautiful," he repeated. "You had a glow about you that attracted me like a magnet. I found myself looking forward to coming home, and that scared me because I was afraid that after the baby was born, you would go back to being the way you were before."

"Well, I didn't," she stated with assurance. "And I don't think I ever will."

The last word was mostly lost in a yawn that came on without warning. She was suddenly very sleepy. The day had been a long one, what with driving and the nervous tension of the confrontation with Burt, which, happily, had ended in understanding between them.

"There's a lot to do the next few days," she mumbled drowsily. "We have to move back into the other house, put this one up for sale, and get married, of course."

A change in his body alerted her that something was wrong even before he spoke, his words piercing her grogginess, but still not clearing her mind.

"You have to contact your ex-husband and tell

him to stop the alimony payments, too," he reminded, his tone indicating how distasteful the subject was to him.

She relaxed, relieved that it hadn't been anything serious after all.

"I've already done that," she said, feeling herself drifting off and struggling to finish the thought. "I called him when I was at Cappy's. He was delighted no end when I told him I hadn't spent a cent of it and would be sending it all back." She yawned again, cavernously this time. "Sorry, darling, but I just can't . . . stay . . . awake . . ."

He hugged her so close she couldn't breathe and then relaxed his hold and kissed her gently on the lips.

"Sleep well, sweetheart. I love you," he said softly.

She smiled in the darkness. He may have thought she was asleep already and wouldn't hear him, but she had! With practice he would eventually say it without shyness and even in front of others, but it would never sound sweeter or more from the heart than this first time!

MORE ROMANCE FOR
A SPECIAL WAY TO RELAX

$1.95 each

2 ☐ Hastings	21 ☐ Hastings	41 ☐ Halston	60 ☐ Thorne
3 ☐ Dixon	22 ☐ Howard	42 ☐ Drummond	61 ☐ Beckman
4 ☐ Vitek	23 ☐ Charles	43 ☐ Shaw	62 ☐ Bright
5 ☐ Converse	24 ☐ Dixon	44 ☐ Eden	63 ☐ Wallace
6 ☐ Douglass	25 ☐ Hardy	45 ☐ Charles	64 ☐ Converse
7 ☐ Stanford	26 ☐ Scott	46 ☐ Howard	65 ☐ Cates
8 ☐ Halston	27 ☐ Wisdom	47 ☐ Stephens	66 ☐ Mikels
9 ☐ Baxter	28 ☐ Ripy	48 ☐ Ferrell	67 ☐ Shaw
10 ☐ Thiels	29 ☐ Bergen	49 ☐ Hastings	68 ☐ Sinclair
11 ☐ Thornton	30 ☐ Stephens	50 ☐ Browning	69 ☐ Dalton
12 ☐ Sinclair	31 ☐ Baxter	51 ☐ Trent	70 ☐ Clare
13 ☐ Beckman	32 ☐ Douglass	52 ☐ Sinclair	71 ☐ Skillern
14 ☐ Keene	33 ☐ Palmer	53 ☐ Thomas	72 ☐ Belmont
15 ☐ James	35 ☐ James	54 ☐ Hohl	73 ☐ Taylor
16 ☐ Carr	36 ☐ Dailey	55 ☐ Stanford	74 ☐ Wisdom
17 ☐ John	37 ☐ Stanford	56 ☐ Wallace	75 ☐ John
18 ☐ Hamilton	38 ☐ John	57 ☐ Thornton	76 ☐ Ripy
19 ☐ Shaw	39 ☐ Milan	58 ☐ Douglass	77 ☐ Bergen
20 ☐ Musgrave	40 ☐ Converse	59 ☐ Roberts	78 ☐ Gladstone

MORE ROMANCE FOR
A SPECIAL WAY TO RELAX

$2.25 each

79 ☐ Hastings	82 ☐ McKenna	85 ☐ Beckman	88 ☐ Saxon
80 ☐ Douglass	83 ☐ Major	86 ☐ Halston	89 ☐ Meriwether
81 ☐ Thornton	84 ☐ Stephens	87 ☐ Dixon	90 ☐ Justin

LOOK FOR *WAY OF THE WILLOW*
BY LINDA SHAW

Silhouette Intimate Moments

Coming Soon

Dreams Of Evening by Kristin James

Tonio Cruz was a part of Erica Logan's past and she hated him for betraying her. Then he walked back into her life and Erica's fear of loving him again was nothing compared to her fear that he would discover the one secret link that still bound them together.

Once More With Feeling by Nora Roberts

Raven and Brand—charismatic, temperamental, talented. Their songs had once electrified the world. Now, after a separation of five years, they were to be reunited to create their special music again. The old magic was still there, but would it be enough to mend two broken hearts?

Emeralds In The Dark by Beverly Bird

Courtney Winston's sight was fading, but she didn't need her eyes to know that Joshua Knight was well worth loving. If only her stubborn pride would let her compromise, but she refused to tie any man to her when she knew that someday he would have to be her eyes.

Sweetheart Contract by Pat Wallace

Wynn Carson, trucking company executive, and Duke Bellini, union president, were on opposite sides of the bargaining table. But once they got together in private, they were very much on the same side.

Silhouette Special Edition

Coming Next Month

Love's Gentle Chains by Sondra Stanford

Lynn had fled from Drew believing she didn't belong in his world. Then she discovered she was bound to him by her love and the child he had unknowingly fathered.

All's Fair by Lucy Hamilton

Automotive engineer Kitty Gordon had been in love with race driver Steve Duncan when she was sixteen. But this time, she would find the inside track to his heart.

Love Feud by Anne Lacey

Carole returned to the hills of North Carolina and rediscovered Jon. His family was still an anathema to hers, but he drew her to him with a sensuous spell she was unable to resist.

Cry Mercy, Cry Love by Monica Barrie

Heather Strand, although blind since birth, saw more clearly than Reid Hunter until love sharpened his vision and he realized that Heather was the only woman for him—forever.

A Matter Of Trust by Emily Doyle

After being used by one man, Victoria Van Straaten wanted to keep Andreas at arm's length. However, on a cruise to Crete she found Andreas determined to close the distance.

Dreams Lost, Dreams Found by Pamela Wallace

It was as though Brynne was reliving a Scottish legend with Ross Fleming—descendant of the Lord of the Isles. Only this time the legend would have a happy ending.